Tegan Bennett Daylight w
She is the author of *Bomb*
listed for the *Australian*/Vo
Kathleen Mitchell Award, and *What Falls Away*
(2001). In 2002 she was named one of the *Sydney Morning Herald*'s Best Young Australian Novelists.

Praise for *Bombora*

'Thank God for Tegan Bennett ... *Bombora* shines like the morning star promising a rosy future for Australian literature ... one of the most exciting and elegantly accomplished pieces of fiction from a young writer that I have read for many years ... Her creation of characters and her mapping of relationships reveal an acute and compassionate understanding of the workings of the human heart and a discerning eye for the infinite subtleties of human behaviour. Hers is a fresh, confident and engaging new literary voice, a cause for both thanks and celebration.' *Vogue*

'A writer of real promise and considerable accomplishment, able to invest her characters with dignity and intelligence, and capable of writing prose that at its best is the equal of Helen Garner or Penelope Lively ... A very impressive debut, a book that in one fell swoop has placed Bennett far ahead of her contemporaries.'
Courier-Mail

'Tegan Bennett is a writer to look out for, no doubt about that ... [her] writing has many strengths – dialogue that conveys the essence of unarticulated emotions; settings that convey a strong sense of place ... narrative that weaves seamlessly back and forth through her characters' lives, striking imagery.' *Australian Book Review*

'Bennett has captured contemporary emotions and relationships with a sense of realism which is both astringent and often hilarious ... She can write pithy observations, create sharply defined characters within stylish, satisfying plots.' *Sydney Morning Herald*

What Falls Away

'One of the most promising writers to hit the Australian literary scene in years.' *Herald Sun*

'Beautiful, intelligent, sensitive writing.' *She*

'[Bennett] is one of the most talented Australian realists to emerge in recent times ... Engaging, well-observed and effortlessly evocative.' *Age*

'There are sentences that read like Jane Austen and others that uncover the magic of the everyday.' *Australian*

'[Bennett] has the coveted gift of compressing emotion into a few lines.' *Canberra Times*

'A quiet gem of understatement, control and subtlety.' *Sun-Herald*

'[Bennett] writes with incisive intelligence ... A brilliant piece of writing.' *The Bulletin*

safety

Tegan Bennett Daylight

𝒱
VINTAGE

A Vintage Book
Published by
Random House Australia Pty Ltd
20 Alfred Street, Milsons Point, NSW 2061
http://www.randomhouse.com.au

Sydney   New York   Toronto
London   Auckland   Johannesburg

First published in Australia in 2006 by Vintage

Australian Government
Australia Council
for the Arts

This project has been assisted by the Australian Government through
the Australia Council, its art funding and advisory body.

National Library of Australia
Cataloguing-in-Publication Entry

Bennett Daylight, Tegan, 1969–.
Safety.

ISBN 1 74051 390 8.

I. Title.

A823.3

Typeset in 12/15 pt Granjon by Midland Typesetters, Australia
Printed and bound by Griffin Press, Netley, South Australia

10 9 8 7 6 5 4 3 2 1

for Russell

The author gratefully acknowledges the support of Varuna, The Writers' House and the Literature Board of the Australia Council during the writing of this book.

I don't know how much pain the bull is in, nor when its shock may spin into injury, nor even when an animal may 'feel' such things, but I do appear to be observing considerable distress – distress which seems to remove the possibility of the corrida's promised artistry ever making an appearance. I also can't help noticing the black joke, winking under it all – the constant portrayal of the innocent entering an unknown world, being punished for its own nature: the greater the promise, the deeper the wounds.

A. L. Kennedy, *On Bullfighting*

When they were fifteen, Elizabeth and her friend Rita sneaked into the big, high-walled boys' college that stood on the edge of their suburb. It was nearly Christmas, and the college had already broken up for the year. Elizabeth and Rita still had another week of school, but it was easy to leave at lunchtime, ducking as they passed the low windows of the English staffroom, and walk up the main road to the boys' college.

The girls paused at the gates, hands flat on the cool sandstone, looking in. The grounds were green and silent. The walls seemed to hold off the sounds of traffic and cicadas, the quivering heat of the afternoon.

Elizabeth followed Rita through the gates. They could hear their sandals squashing on the gravel drive. There was no-one about, although you could imagine a monk hurrying over the grass, head down, hands folded together inside his sleeves.

They crossed the lawn and walked past the long swimming pool, its blue water ruffling in the breeze. Elizabeth stopped, entranced. It was a hot day. She would have liked to run and fling herself at its centre, hitting the water with a crack, and sinking to see the batik of light on the blue tiles.

Rita was at the other end of the pool, beckoning her. 'Come on,' she hissed. 'That's it,' she said, pointing at a long, two-storey building.

A man appeared around the corner of the building. They stood still. He did have a monk's look; intent, head down, he crossed the grass without seeing them, and was gone. Somewhere a sprinkler ticked.

The big building had double doors which were wide open, leading to a flight of stairs. They slipped in. It was cooler inside, and darker. Rita led them up, the stairs creaking underfoot. The wood smelt of furniture polish.

'I think this is the one.'

The room was long, and striped with dusty sunlight. The walls were lined with barred windows which gave a prisoner's view of the green and geometrical grounds. Under each window was a bed. Beside each bed was a chest of drawers, with a lamp on it.

Elizabeth and Rita stared and stared.

'Do you think the older guys sleep here?' said Elizabeth.

'I don't know,' said Rita. 'I thought they had studies and stuff. And fags.'

They each stifled a laugh.

'Which one's his?'

Rita shook her head. 'I can't remember.'

A noise on the stair behind them catapulted them forward into the long room. Elizabeth stumbled and nearly fell, but Rita grabbed her hand, pulling her up. Somebody called out as they bolted for the far door, their feet thundering on the boards. The beds flashed past them. They were giggling without control as they started down the opposite set of stairs.

They slipped and slid in the gravel; Rita was laughing as she shoved Elizabeth through the tall gates, and then overtook her, running ahead to the lights. She stopped and thumped a hand on the crossing button. Elizabeth caught up, gasping, and had to lean on the pole.

'Do you think they saw our uniforms?' said Elizabeth.

'I don't know,' panted Rita.

'They might come down to the school straight away,' said Elizabeth, her hand on her throat.

The lights changed, and they stepped into the road. 'Don't worry,' said Rita. 'They'll never know it was us.'

Rita was killed in a car accident when they were seventeen, driving down Parramatta Road with her boyfriend, long after midnight when the road was empty of other cars. Elizabeth had been with them before on such a night. Rita's boyfriend took the four

3

lanes of dark road, white lines glittering in the street-lights, as a challenge. He boasted that once he'd reached a hundred and fifty on the hill down to Ashfield. This time, however, it was raining. He lost control of the car, spinning them into an empty Korean restaurant, its front window shattering around them. They were killed as they slammed into the restaurant's side wall.

On the first Monday after the accident Elizabeth and her friends did not know how to talk to each other about what had happened. Teenage life, with all its exaggeration, its shrieks and hysteria, is not built to accommodate real sorrow. The girls could hardly meet each other's eyes – they walked to assembly together but not touching, shouldering their bags and looking straight ahead. When the headmaster told the school about the 'tragedy' that had occurred on the weekend they shifted a little closer to each other, but still did not touch.

Three nights later there was a storm and Elizabeth woke up to feel rain on her face. She sat up in bed to close her window. It was pouring; when she pulled the window shut the willow tree thrashed wet handfuls of leaves against the glass. Elizabeth stared out, thinking of Rita's body at the cemetery, in its box. She climbed back into bed and lay with the covers pulled up tight. Rita would have her hands by her sides, her eyes closed.

Rita faded too quickly as the days passed, like the lightprint left of someone when you close your eyes on their image. She had always laughed in class (she could not be stopped, she was always being sent out); she sat up the back; she was a daring and aggressive netball player; she wore sneakers instead of school shoes.

Elizabeth would remember the smaller, more private things: how Rita had talked about losing her virginity. Her boyfriend had stayed the night and they'd had a shower together. Elizabeth could not even begin to imagine this. How she had been on the bus after school, looked up and seen two girls staring at her and whispering to each other. One of them had actually said, *Isn't she ugly*. Rita had told this story quickly, not allowing Elizabeth to say anything.

Coming down the stairs the next morning, Elizabeth overheard her mother discussing the accident on the phone. Were they wearing seatbelts? Nobody seemed to think so. Had they been killed 'instantly', as everyone hoped? Or had they taken Rita to the hospital, where she'd died?

Elizabeth stood still at the bottom of the stairs.

'When I think,' her mother said, 'if Elizabeth had been with them. Well, I can't bear to think about it.'

Elizabeth cleared her throat.

'I just hope they felt no *pain*,' said her mother.

Elizabeth cleared her throat again and her mother said, 'I'll have to go.'

She hugged Elizabeth when she came into the kitchen but Elizabeth could not respond, and stood with her face squashed against her mother's shoulder, which smelt of White Linen. It was too hard to know how to show grief. Should she be angry? Should she allow herself to be found in private corners of the house, weeping? Was it wrong to eat? She was not used to being noticed so significantly by her parents, and could not think how to temper her behaviour to the sudden beam of their attention.

When her mother released her she went over to the kitchen cupboard and took out the Weetbix. She wondered if braver people died and more timid ones remained in the world. And if, now that this brave person was gone, her own days of risk-taking were over. She should keep quiet now, and still, in case something snatched her up and took her away.

Elizabeth was not a good driver. Her oldest sister had taught her, taking her out after school, but Elizabeth hated the feel of the car underneath her, of its reckless weighted surge when she pressed the accelerator with her foot. She had learned to drive because it was expected of her, and her parents were ready to pass on her sisters' old car. But after Rita died Elizabeth stopped driving altogether. Nobody noticed. Her middle sister Charlotte was still at home, and although she had a boyfriend with a car, she was glad to be able to use the old blue Gemini.

It was possible to move unseen through the house, to come and go as she wanted. Her parents had given up watching their children, and Elizabeth seemed so docile compared with her sisters. She wasn't the kind of girl to take risks. Elizabeth could remember holding her mother's hand at parties and hearing her mother whisper above her head, *Shy*.

Her mother, who was the house's biggest presence, spent most of her time on the phone, her need to communicate clearly overwhelming. She would stop cooking and rush to the phone if she'd thought of something to say – put a hand on your knee to silence you if she thought she heard the phone ring downstairs. It was possible to walk right by her without her seeing you when she was on the phone; Charlotte had once proved this with a whole bottle of expensive gin. Elizabeth's mother did not care if Elizabeth went out on foot or by car, was picked up by someone or stayed in her room. She mostly stayed in her room, the radio on, her books open in front of her.

Charlotte, who was still at home because she was always saving for holidays with her boyfriend, had a party when their parents were safely away for the weekend. The word passed much faster than she expected it to, so that nearly a hundred people showed up. Elizabeth sat at the bottom of the wooden stairs, where she'd sat so often to do up her school shoes, or to trap their wriggling cat in her arms. She clutched a wine cooler and tried to talk herself into joining the people who were dancing on the blue carpet of the living room. Her mother's chairs were all pulled back against the walls. In one of them a boy and girl lay, their faces hidden by the chair's deep arms. Elizabeth was taking another lukewarm swallow of her sweet drink when she saw one of Charlotte's old school-friends, Richard, detach himself from a group of boys. He came up to her, made her move over on the bottom step, and sat down.

Richard was three years older than she was. He had tanned skin, blond hair and a girl's mouth, dark-lipped and smiling. Elizabeth knew him, in the odd way you know your sister's friends – she had barely spoken to him, but she had watched him from behind a book at the kitchen table, when Charlotte and her friends barged through the house, their competitive talk filling the rooms with noise. She had answered the phone when he rang. And once, she had answered the door when he'd come to pick Charlotte up for a party.

Elizabeth tried to move further away from Richard on the step, not wanting to seem rude. She wondered if he remembered coming to the house that time. She had been fourteen perhaps, at that stage before you become truly aware of your body, and the embarrassment and attention it can cause. Still a child, in Elizabeth's case. There had been a crashing at the door – someone who didn't know not to use the black iron knocker, who hadn't seen the doorbell – and Charlotte, with the Violent Femmes at full volume, hadn't heard it. Elizabeth had been having a bath, lying in the lukewarm water and re-reading *The Silver Brumby*. She'd hauled herself out of the water, reaching for a towel and pulling it around her, not looking at herself in the bathroom's full-length mirror. She left wet footprints on the wooden steps.

When she reached the bottom she could see the shadow of somebody tall, somebody male, in the frosted glass at the top of the door.

She pulled the door open, sure it was some idiot friend of Charlotte's, and of course it was. 'What?' she said rudely.

And Richard, blinking once, had grinned at her, and said nothing.

'You looking for Charlotte?'

He nodded, and she turned her head towards the stairs to screech, 'CHARLOTTE!', and when she turned back, Richard was still grinning at her.

'What?' she said again, and he nodded, used his head to gesture at her towel, which she still clutched around her. She glanced down. Her breasts were covered, as they were meant to be, but the towel gaped open at the bottom, and all Richard needed to do was duck his head and he could see between her legs. She stared at him, horrified, and pulled the towel more closely around her, so tightly that as she backed away she almost tripped. 'I'll get Charlotte,' she said, and scurried back up the stairs as fast as the hobbling towel would let her.

And now she was seventeen and Richard's shoulder was warm as he moved closer again. He spoke gently, quietly, as though he had something private to say to her, though what he said was hardly new.

'Haven't seen you round for ages,' he said.

'I've had exams,' said Elizabeth.

Richard said nothing, allowing the silence to gather between them, long enough to make Elizabeth deeply uncomfortable. She could feel herself about to ask him what he'd got in his HSC out of sheer desperation, when he said, 'I mean I haven't seen you for years.'

'Then you haven't been looking,' said Elizabeth.

He turned to her and smiled; he said, 'I wish I had been,' and put his hand on her arm. He nudged her gaze upwards with his own eyes, forcing her to meet them. Elizabeth was much too inexperienced to recognise a technique; she watched him, feeling her heart beat, as he walked away. She saw the expectant grins on his friends' faces as he reached them, but their meaning did not register. One of them slapped him on the back.

He must have slept downstairs on one of the couches, because when she came down to the kitchen in the morning he was there, sitting at the counter, reading the newspaper that he had collected from the front step and unrolled. The sticky plastic wrapping was on the floor.

'Hi,' said Elizabeth. He smiled at her, saying nothing.

She went to the fridge. She looked in. Her mother had bought extra milk, thinking that they might have friends to stay. There was a row of white bottles on the bottom shelf of the fridge. None of them had been opened. She took one out and carried it over to the counter where Richard sat. She reached up to the cupboard and took out a glass. Richard kept reading. She shook the bottle of milk, peeled off the foil cap and poured herself a full glass, which she drank, watching him read the paper.

Two people Elizabeth did not know – a tall, dark-skinned boy with his hair shaved at the sides and back, a pile of messy, bleached curls on top, and a girl wearing a pair of Charlotte's pyjamas – walked through the kitchen. Richard turned around.

'You still here?' said the dark boy.

'Too drunk to drive,' said Richard.

They came and sat down at the counter with Richard.

Elizabeth stared at them. 'I live here, you know,' she said.

The pyjamaed girl looked at her, and then, as though Elizabeth had said something too rude to acknowledge, looked away and leaned back into her boyfriend's arms. 'I feel terrible,' she announced.

Elizabeth set down her glass, the white film sinking to the bottom. She would have liked to make a cup of tea, but she could not bring herself to turn her back on the three of them.

'We met last night,' Richard said to her. 'I'm Richard.'

'I know,' said Elizabeth. The morning was already warm, and she could feel sweat starting under her arms and beneath her breasts.

'Do you want to come for a walk with me?' said Richard.

'Have you got any coffee?' said the pyjamaed girl.

Elizabeth slid the jar of instant towards her. 'Okay,' she said to Richard.

Her suburb, seen in the dazed blue light of a hangover, seemed unfamiliar. She kept a metre or so between herself and Richard, so that he could not take her hand. This walk, this promise of intimacy, was what she had wanted, but now that she had it she was not sure. His closeness made her feel ill. She hoped she wouldn't vomit. She could taste the wine coolers, and the milk slopping in her stomach.

He touched her for the first time when they reached the park, not waiting for her to turn her body to his. Her skin jumped, alive with little shocks. They were sitting on some rocks, still cool in the shade, though the dewy grass had dried and the city was beginning to shimmer in the distance.

Elizabeth resisted Richard's large warm hand as it reached into her shirt, feeling for her breast; she took hold of the hand, trying to force it away, but he forced back. His fingers found their way into her bra. Elizabeth froze.

'Come on,' said Richard, moving closer to her. In the distance she saw her next-door neighbours, walking their dog at the very edge of the oval, too far away to recognise her. Then Richard covered her view of them, and she closed her eyes as his mouth opened on hers.

She couldn't talk when they got back to her house; wordlessly, she ran into the garden, leaving Richard to shut the gate behind them. She didn't look back as she crossed the bottle-strewn yard and went into the house. She wanted to close the front door on him and stand against it, but had enough sense to see that that was not reasonable. Instead, she ran up to her parents' room, hoping he would not follow her, and sat on the edge of their bed, her heart beating. The open door felt like a terrible threat; the stairs yawned at her. After ten minutes she leaned over to her mother's side, picked up her discarded paperback and began reading.

Elizabeth knew that she was an innocent, compared with other girls her own age, and compared with her sisters. Virginia, the oldest, always the steady one, had had boyfriends since she was fifteen. Nice boys; even Elizabeth could see that. Grinning nervously at her parents when they came to visit, not touching Virginia in front of her family. Elizabeth loved Virginia – the five years' distance between them made this possible without competition. Virginia was serene, and happy, and kind. She and her boyfriends had let Elizabeth hang around with them when she was eleven or twelve, and the boys were always nice enough – or young enough – to watch *Countdown* with her, or to play games in the pool. But once Elizabeth, having run back to the house for her flippers, had returned to find Virginia and one of her boyfriends wrapped around each other at the edge of the pool, their faces moving together. Virginia looked up and caught sight of Elizabeth, and jerked away from Peter, her cheeks and mouth stained red as though she had been eating strawberries.

'Elizabeth!' she called, and Elizabeth, more embarrassed than she would ever care to remember, did not know what to do. She stared at them; Virginia started to stand up, and Elizabeth turned and ran, like a fool, with the cold flippers slapping against her leg. She skirted the sunny western wall of the house and ducked behind the azaleas in the front garden, where she crouched, gasping. Virginia ran past, calling her name, but Elizabeth kept still, trying to silence her breathing until finally Virginia shrugged and walked off.

By the time Charlotte had grown into having boyfriends, Elizabeth had schooled herself out of this extreme sensibility, or the appearance of it at least, and made herself disdainful of sex. Charlotte, on the other hand, threw herself into it, in a way that Elizabeth could only secretly envy. One night Elizabeth was woken by a groaning and shouting under her bedroom window, which was next to Charlotte's. There was a boy on the lawn, obviously drunk, staggering and putting his hand out against the air as though it was a wall that might hold him upright. 'Char-lotte!' he bawled.

Elizabeth pulled up her window and leaned out, saying, 'Go home, dickhead.'

The boy was drunk enough to mistake her for her sister. 'Come down here,' he moaned, like a stupid dog. 'I wanna talk to you.'

Charlotte's window went up. She put her head out, glanced sideways at Elizabeth and then hissed at the boy, 'What are you doing here? It's two in the morning!'

'I wanna talk to you,' groaned the boy. He stepped back; his legs buckled under him and he sat down heavily on the lawn. Charlotte and Elizabeth looked at each other.

'I'll go down,' said Charlotte. 'He'll wake Mum and Dad. Go back to bed.' Elizabeth could see her eyes glinting in the dark.

'Don't let him come upstairs. They'll spew. Or he will.'

'Of course I won't, idiot.' Charlotte pulled her window down, careful not to let it bang.

Elizabeth was too cool to care what Charlotte did with her boyfriends, but when she got back in bed her heart was ticking over fast. And it took a long time to fall asleep again, lying in the dappled dark of the streetlight and listening for Charlotte's and her boyfriend's voices.

She could not let anyone know this, but she dreamed of sex, and wished that it could happen as if it was a dream, a coupling of bodies freed of flesh and thought. She and Rita had spoken about this, both hoping for that rush of hot unfumbling passion that would deliver them from virginity without pain or knowledge. But how was this to be found in the arms of hostile, uncertain schoolboys, who only wanted to have done, to struggle free of the act and tell their friends? Elizabeth could not trust herself to them, and Rita would leave her behind, in more ways than one.

Elizabeth was the third child, born when her mother was still toilet-training Charlotte, still pre-occupied with Virginia's first days at school. Benignly neglected, some children grow up careless, confident of their ability to look after themselves. Others become their own parents; they learn to guard themselves. Elizabeth tried to keep herself safe, though from what she was never certain. Sex had always seemed dangerous; this was a time when teenagers did not talk about it, except to compete, in a veiled sort of way, about loss of virginity. No-one knew who had really done it, but everyone pretended to, even Elizabeth. So no-one really knew what it was like until they summoned the courage – or got drunk enough – to give it a go.

With Richard it had been fumbling; his hands on the straps of her bra, and then pulling her shorts down. The sight of her right foot as Richard laboured on top of her, shorts and underpants dangling from it. The pain, which she had been so frightened of, like a sore knee, but nothing more.

Richard didn't call afterwards, but Elizabeth was glad. It would have been too much. When her period finally came she was speechless with relief. She lay in bed all day, feeling the blood come warmly out of her, and tears trickling easily down the sides of her face. In the following weeks, when she got up in the sunny mornings and went downstairs, she couldn't think why she had been so worried. Everybody had sex. You couldn't get pregnant the first time. She felt as though she had got away with it. The house and her suburb became themselves again; everything looked simple and primary-coloured, like a children's book. It would have been easy to walk through the streets with him now. She was washed with shame when she thought about hiding in her parents' bedroom. She had finished her mother's book, listening to the sounds of cars leaving, of Charlotte leaning out of her bedroom window and screaming with laughter. She'd sat there till her neck ached and the house was silent, except for the miaows of the unfed cat at the back door.

Elizabeth finished her exams, and found herself swinging in space. Her friendships, once full of a breathless tension – the long, passionate conversations about The Cure, about the English exam, about the beautiful punk boy who caught the same bus, to some-where unimaginable – came apart like an old rubber band. As though they had agreed on it earlier, she and her friends stopped phoning each other. They had nothing to say anymore.

Encouraged by Charlotte, who worked in a gift shop, Elizabeth found herself a job in a bakery, in a small shopping centre a few suburbs away. She started work at five am. When she got there (eyes stinging in the fluorescent light, walking past shop after shut-tered shop until she reached the very bowels of the centre) the bakers would be listening to music at top volume. They had been up all night. They'd had lines of speed at the beginning of their shift; by the time Elizabeth arrived they would be lighting joints. They were red-eyed, manic, grinning and shrieking to the music. They offered Elizabeth a drag, or a line. She was too shy to say yes.

One of them was not much older than her; he was quieter than the others, with curly light brown hair and blue eyes like semi-precious stones, not yet ruined by the mad hours he worked. Sometimes, being an apprentice, he served at the counter with Elizabeth. When he bent down to get something, he would tickle the backs of Elizabeth's knees, trying to make her laugh in front of the customers.

She was working with Mark on the day that Richard turned up. She saw him at the back of the crowd of customers and her heart dropped, a cool sweat beginning on her shoulders and neck. Richard moved forward as Mark served the woman ahead of him. He was smiling his pleased, curved smile.

'Charlotte told me you'd be here,' he said, before she could open her mouth.

She ducked her head. She was thrilled, and terrified.

'I wondered what you were doing on New Year's Eve,' he said.

'I don't know,' said Elizabeth.

He smiled again. 'Do you want to come out with me? There's a couple of parties.'

'Okay,' said Elizabeth.

'I'll give you a call,' said Richard, and left, without buying anything.

'Who's that?' said Mark. He shifted slightly so that his shoulder touched hers.

'A friend of my sister's,' said Elizabeth. She was hot now. She could see herself reflected in the window of the shop opposite, her dyed and spiked hair bright above her face. She was much shorter than Mark. Elizabeth put a hand up to wipe her forehead, which was greasy from the butter and oil and pastry, and Mark said, 'What did he want?'

Richard picked her up every day after work, and Mark didn't tickle the backs of her knees anymore. The bakers seemed sour and resentful, and no longer offered her a joint for the pleasure of seeing it turned down. Someone lost the Sunnyboys tape, and they were shouting Midnight Oil songs when she got to work, and pretending to bang their heads on the long chrome counters.

Sex with Richard was no longer terrifying. He was an intense boy, given to seizing her hands and staring into her eyes; undoing her jeans in the car on the way home because he was 'desperate' for her; telling her there was nothing so soft as her skin.

'I thought all girls' skin was soft,' she said.

He shook his head. They were lying on his bed in the flat he shared with friends in North Sydney – a cold city light barged into the uncurtained room. 'Yours is the softest I have ever touched,' he whispered, giving the impression he'd had a fleet of lovers before her. He rolled on top of her.

Elizabeth nearly always wanted to have sex – it was so exciting, the start of it, his hands on her breasts and his mouth pushing hers open – but each time was left stranded. Richard believed in the vaginal orgasm. He explained it to her. He read her a passage from a Norman Mailer book that described it. He knew she could achieve it through the intensity of their love-making, and once or twice Elizabeth pretended to, making her breath quicken the way it did when she was alone, catching excitedly as Richard gasped on top of her.

But each time Elizabeth lay rigidly awake when they had finished. She could not ask Richard to do anything. It would be too embarrassing. She pressed a hand between her legs but could not move it for fear of waking Richard up. Sometimes she simply fell asleep without even being aware of it, drifting off as she stared out of the window. But other times she lay there, rage and frustration building, with Richard breathing ignorantly next to her. She wanted to scream or to hit him with something. But there was nothing to hit him with, and she never did.

The last time she saw Richard was in Queensland, during the Easter holidays. They were camping with a group of his friends in a tiny, fibro town where the blue water glittered as it tumbled on the sand. Dolphins patrolled the bays every morning and every evening, appearing just when you thought you'd missed them, their grey backs like sudden rocky outcrops in the blue.

Charlotte was there, with her boyfriend: they slept with the group in a big, house-like tent that one of the more earnest boys owned. Richard had brought a one-boy tent from his days at the boys' college, the same place that Elizabeth and Rita had stolen into on that hot afternoon. At the boys' college they were all forced to join the cadets and go camping, making fires and cooking beans in a tin.

When Elizabeth and Richard got into the tent, it bulged. Any movement they made threatened to split its sides.

'We'll have to sleep close together,' said Richard, taking Elizabeth by the ankle as she scrambled out in front of him. She kicked but could not free herself; he pulled her back in and kissed her on her neck. He had an odd way of kissing; a downward movement, like someone taking a bite out of an apple.

They spent the night drinking at the bowling club, which was on the cliff above the water. The beer was very cheap. Everyone got drunk. They stumbled down the hill towards the camping ground. It was still and hot, as though summer had not passed; there was a huge orange moon, hanging in the sky and casting its thoughtful light across the stippled surface of the sea.

'It's too fucking hot in this tent!' shouted Charlotte's boyfriend when they got back, after losing themselves, staggering around and incurring groans of rage from the other people at the camping ground. 'Less sleep under the stars!'

They all dragged their lilos and sleeping bags out, shrieking with laughter and tripping over each other.

'Our tent'll be alright,' said Richard, appearing behind Elizabeth. 'It's more private.'

Richard wanted to have sex, but this time Elizabeth was not sure. 'We can't,' she whispered. 'They're just out there. They'll be able to hear everything.'

'They won't even know,' said Richard. 'They're too pissed.'

'Richard –' said Elizabeth, pushing his hands away. They were both sweating.

'Don't be stupid,' he said. 'They're all asleep.'

They stopped, and listened. No-one was talking.

'They can hear everything,' hissed Elizabeth, as Richard slid his hand into her underpants. 'Don't!' She pinched him, hard, on the arm.

Richard's closed hand came down on the side of her face solidly, but soundlessly. Elizabeth gasped and turned her face so that the next blow caught her on the nose, making her eyes fill with tears. Through them she could see Richard looking at her. This time she lifted her body obediently as Richard tugged at her underpants, holding herself up so that he could pull them down her legs. He climbed on top of her. She did not try to push him away, but he pinned her arms with his hands anyway.

'Don't,' whispered Elizabeth. She closed her eyes and held herself in. She even clenched her legs around

Richard, trying to keep his pushing, his moving, to a minimum. What if everyone was standing outside laughing silently, seeing the tent about to split. This was the worst thing. It was so hot. She could feel sweat under her back. She tried to keep very still, and tried to stop breathing as his weight pressed into her. When his face came close to hers she whispered again, 'Don't let them hear.'

She lay awake until Richard was deeply asleep, too young yet to snore with drunkenness, his gorgeous face tilted to one side. Then – holding her breath at the shh shh of her skin against the tent – she slid out, feet first. She had not cried, but her face was stiff, as if she had, and her legs were sticky and shaking. She picked her way through the sleeping bodies – their faces illuminated by the moon, which was now autumnally pale and higher in the sky, out of reach – and over to the big tent. Her bag was inside. She packed it, not knowing if she grabbed her own clothes or the others', and groped back to the entrance. She sat there, bag on her knees, until the moon slid down the sky and the dawn light began to wash into the dark of the sea.

She found Charlotte. She was lying on her stomach, one arm thrown over her boyfriend.

'Hey,' Elizabeth whispered, shaking her.

Charlotte shifted, and turned away from her boy-friend. She opened her eyes and saw Elizabeth. Her face was blotchy. 'Whassup?'

'I've got to go home.'

'What?' Charlotte lifted her head, pushing the hair out of her eyes. It was still quite dark. Elizabeth looked down, and away from Charlotte. 'It's okay,' she whispered, 'I've just got to go.'

'What happened? How will you get home?'

'Nothing. I'll walk into town and get the train.'

Charlotte was trying to get out of her sleeping bag. Elizabeth put a hand on her shoulder to stop her.

'But you might have to wait all day!' said Charlotte.

'I'll get the early one. Don't worry. I'm all set to go.'

'What about Richard?'

'I broke up with him.'

Charlotte understood this – the need to be gone. 'Have you got enough money?' she said. Her boyfriend shifted in his sleep and she put a quieting hand on his hair.

'Yeah. I'll see you at home.'

Charlotte nodded. She watched Elizabeth thread her way through the camping ground, and, when Elizabeth glanced back, raised her hand to wave. Then Elizabeth saw her wriggle back down into her sleeping bag, and disappear from view.

Faced again with Elizabeth's disappearance, Richard did not call. For weeks afterwards Elizabeth braced herself every time the phone rang. Whenever she thought about the scene with Richard she felt nauseated with shame. None of Charlotte's friends had mentioned it, but she could not be sure that they hadn't heard. She wondered what Richard was thinking. She didn't know what she would say if he did ring, but he didn't, and Elizabeth denied herself the opportunity of talking about him by telling Charlotte never to mention his name again.

'Okay,' Charlotte said, shrugging, and got up to change the channel on the tv.

Elizabeth knew there was a problem with having tried to imitate Charlotte, who lived as though she was in a movie. If such a thing had happened to Charlotte – though how could it? – she too would have forbidden anyone to mention Richard's name. But then within a week she would have had a better, nicer boyfriend and Richard would have seen them together and regretted his meanness, and regretted not calling, and felt punished.

But Elizabeth was not a proper girl, not in the sense that Charlotte and her lipsticked friends were. Charlotte even looked more like a girl than Elizabeth did – where Elizabeth was virtually flat-chested, Charlotte had proper breasts. She had longer, sleeker hair that could be managed into ponytails, and skin that welcomed make-up, smooth and creamy. She and her friends loved games like this one. Charlotte had once held out on her boyfriend for three whole weeks when he offended her, returning his calls only after a huge bunch of carnations, like horrible little frilled brains, was delivered to the house.

At least Elizabeth did not have to talk about it. As long as Richard remained absent, stayed out of sight, she could leave it alone. She could even choose not to think about it. She believed that after a while even the thoughts would fade and disappear.

In the months before she met Ross, when she was in her late twenties and working at the same university where she'd done her degree, Elizabeth slept with several different men, none of whom she liked, let alone loved. The sex they had felt like two people trying to push past each other in a crowd; when they had grappled briefly, they moved on, not looking back. Elizabeth was skilled at slipping out of beds in the early hours, gathering her clothes and dressing in unfamiliar bathrooms, shutting front doors behind her with the faintest of clicks. She never picked up the phone without screening first. There was a sweet moment of relief when the answering machine repeated its message and then the person at the other end hung up without speaking, beeps echoing through the house.

One sunny Sunday Elizabeth was lying on her flatmate Lucy's unmade bed, looking out of the window at the unfamiliar view, its square of pale blue occasionally divided by a slow-moving plane. There was a knock at the door downstairs, and somebody called, 'Hello?' through the barred window of the living room. Instantly Elizabeth knew it was the man she had slept with the week before. She could not remember giving him her address.

She lay still, waiting for him to go away.

'Hello?' he said again, and there was the sound of the door being pushed open. The lock was loose; Lucy was always failing to pull it to properly, in her rush out the door to work, or to her boyfriend's house.

'Hello?' The man was standing in their living room. The right thing to do would have been to get out of bed and go downstairs. Rubbing her eyes, saying, 'Sorry, I was asleep!' But what would that lead to? In bed with the man Elizabeth had been drunk, had let him hold both her wrists above her head. It made her skin prickle to think about it. Quickly, she wriggled under Lucy's enormous doona, pulling it over her head, kicking at its folds to make it look bulky but unoccupied. She heard the man cross the floor of the living room and go out to the kitchen and the courtyard. He was taking a look around, though surely believing there was no-one at home. Elizabeth felt suddenly frightened.

'Anyone here?' said the man, to satisfy his conscience, as he started up the stairs. Elizabeth lay as still as she could under the doona, breathing in her own hot breath. She was grateful for the laziness that had prevented Lucy from buying a new mattress, one that did not sag in the middle. She was sweating lightly all over.

'Elizabeth?' said the man, standing in the hall between the two bedrooms. He came to the doorway of Lucy's room. If he found her, could she pretend to have been asleep?

She held her breath while she felt him stand there, imagining him looking out of the window at the pale sky. An aeroplane, a distant one, dragged past. Elizabeth's heart started to leap in her chest as she heard the man pass Lucy's bedroom, move down the hall to her own room and then, defeated, start down the stairs again. She stayed perfectly still as he pulled the door to. She could hear him carefully making sure that he left it in the same position, not quite closed. She heard the click of his lighter as he stood on their doorstep. She heard him walk away.

There was a cool rush of air as she sat up, flinging the doona off. Her breath was coming in short, painful little gasps.

Elizabeth never told anyone about Richard; not friends, not men, not her sisters or her parents. It was easy. Nobody asked – why would they? – and the memory was too humiliating to be resurrected. It wasn't the kind of story her friends confessed to each other after a few drinks, taking the sting out of small defeats and failures. When she thought about telling she was afraid that people would take it too seriously; she was afraid that people would not take it seriously enough. Was it normal, was it common, what had happened? Was it a big deal, or was it nothing at all? It was an effort to remember, really, to piece it together properly.

Richard had been a symptom, perhaps, rather than a cause of the selfconsciousness she felt during sex, and the shame she felt if she allowed herself to move freely, to forget herself. It had to do with watching herself. To be unguarded was to be vulnerable. But it was easy to have sex without making yourself vulnerable; oddly, sex could be safe, an act without intimacy.

Elizabeth had a brief relationship with a boy who eventually and unsurprisingly confessed that he was gay. The sex they had was barely there – each of them keeping still, hoping that the other would take control, until they spent most nights lying on top of the covers, talking. Craig had been to an expensive country boarding school. Later he told her that he'd once given another boy a blowjob behind the altar in the school chapel. He told her, too, about the Bachelor and Spinster Balls held in the final year of school, in someone's paddock, where the beer came in kegs, the boys wore tuxedos and the girls bright shiny dresses with big skirts that got ruined in the mud.

Craig always went to the parties, afraid to be seen setting himself apart – and always ended up alone, sitting on the boot of someone's car with a bottle of Brandivino or Southern Comfort. At the last party of the year everyone was beside themselves, drinking then vomiting, then drinking again. And Craig, once again alone at the edge of the circle, watching kids dance and smooch by the fire, saw seven boys fucking a girl who had passed out.

'She was on the tray of a ute,' said Craig. 'They just pushed up her dress and went for it. They took turns.'

Elizabeth stared out of her window, at the familiar glimmer of stars.

'I wonder what she thought the next morning,' said Craig. He reached for Elizabeth's hand but she moved it away.

'Why didn't you do anything?' said Elizabeth.

They turned their heads towards each other. Their faces were clear in the dark. 'They would have beaten the shit out of me,' said Craig.

'You should have got someone's parents.' Elizabeth felt a stone of rage in her throat, hard and sharp.

'I was too scared.'

Elizabeth and Craig stopped seeing each other soon after that but, as is the way in Sydney, ran into each other often. They always smiled shyly at each other, a little ashamed at their sexual failure. Once Craig introduced his boyfriend to her in a bar and then drifted off, leaving them together. The boyfriend was brittle, joyful, stupid. 'Isn't Craig gorgeous! And he is a *fox* in the *sack*!' he said to Elizabeth, and took her arm, looking eagerly into her face.

Elizabeth's house was close to the city, her suburb thick with tiny houses and pubs, and air that settled dirtily on the window-frames. In summer the tarred pavements stung with heat. You could not walk barefoot, unless you leapt from shadow to shadow, though they were hard to find under the vertical summer sun. The main road would be jammed with traffic heading east to the beach, the air shimmering with petrol.

She met Ross at Victoria Park pool. Elizabeth left the university after class to swim, avoiding lunch or conversation with her colleagues; it seemed that Ross was doing the same. She knew who he was. He also taught in the communications degree; like her, and so many others, he was casual, coming in for classes but rarely occupying his office. She had seen him running along the corridor, late for work, as she unlocked her classroom door and ushered her students in. Sometimes they stood in the lift together, but they never spoke. Elizabeth hated talking in the lifts; the way the confined space made your words swell, ridiculous against the sound of people breathing, or a student's headphones crashing softly in their ears. She always held her folders against her chest and stared silently at the row of buttons until she reached her floor.

She began to see him, once or twice a week, as she carried her towel across the grass to a position by the back fence. She wondered if he recognised her from the university. He watched her as she passed, and sometimes he smiled.

It was so hot, a sky pulsing with blue, ringing with blue. Elizabeth sat on the tiled edge of the pool, dangling her legs in the warm water, goggles in one hand. A Koori kid lay on his stomach on the concrete, face to one side, smiling to himself, looking like an advertisement for a better Australia. Beyond him, a group of Lebanese boys were clumped on the grass, shouting and smoking. The woman behind the counter of the kiosk propped her chin on her hands, looking out. Towels and bags sat on the long row of steps like musical notes in a child's piece. A dog, slumped at the very end of its leash, watched its owner doing laps: all the way up, and all the way back.

She felt the air become softer next to her and Ross sat down. 'Wanna race?' he said.

Ross was tall, with black hair that would curl if it grew long. He had a soft, bulky body, and skin that smelt sweet and dry. He had brown eyes and hair on his chest. He had a sore shoulder from hunching over his books; talking, he would raise an arm above his head, trying to stretch the muscles.

They ate dinner together that night, in a pub down the road from Elizabeth's house. There had been no southerly yet; the air sweated whenever they moved. Elizabeth sat opposite Ross on a wooden bench, her beer bottle frosted and dripping, her breasts and stomach wet with heat. They drank three, four, five beers. They ate food with whole chillies in it. Elizabeth bit down on one and her mouth began to sing and burn. She looked around the beer garden at the laughing faces of people and felt as if she was floating. But she did not feel drunk.

When they stood up Ross held a hand out to her and she took it. He tucked her arm around him as they left. This was the first time they had touched, but Elizabeth didn't notice it as new. When they stopped in a dark little park to kiss, there was no fumbling or uncertainty. When they broke apart they didn't speak, until Elizabeth said, 'Let's go home,' and Ross, taking her hand again, agreed.

Later that night they walked from Elizabeth's house to the pool, moving through the breezeless air. Ross helped Elizabeth climb the fence where there was a gap in the barbed wire. Once over, they took off all their clothes and slid in. The water felt like a long, cool muscle, gripping Elizabeth's body gently as she dived under and swam along the bottom. Ross swam behind her. They came to the surface, gasping. He kissed her neck and slid his hands up her body to her breasts.

Ross lived out of the inner city, by the river. When Elizabeth stayed at his house she travelled in to work on the ferry, sitting outside to watch the water glitter and rush by the rails. She walked from the Quay to the university. It did not seem to take her very long; she slipped easily and swiftly through the crowds of commuters. The glimpses she caught of herself in the shop windows of George Street were of someone on whom light seemed to have fallen. She laughed at this thought, and saw herself doing so as she strode past the glass walls of a bank.

It was as though she had moved suddenly from a cold climate to a warmer one. Her body, so distant and unfamiliar for such a long time, began to make sense. It continued to respond to Ross. She had skin. It no longer smelt of chlorine, or smoke, or perfume. Now it smelt of salt, and something sweet, which she could taste on her forearm (bringing it to her mouth one day, sucking it as she would a peach).

She had forgotten what it was like to walk in a garden, or with bare feet, except on the clammy carpets in her neglected house. Outside Ross's front door a Norfolk Island hibiscus dropped its seed pods, which split to spread a thousand tiny, prickling hairs. They caught in your feet, between your toes. You had to lean over and brush gently at the skin, trying for the little snag of a hair. Elizabeth, holding her ankle in one hand, looked at the smooth white skin of her foot and pressed a thumb deep into the arch. There were parts of her that had not been touched for years.

She felt newly wealthy, as though by contact with Ross she had become invulnerable to bills, to the price of luxury. She spent recklessly, bringing home a bottle of wine from the twenty dollar rack, a book, a new dress that had slithered easily onto her body in the shop. Two turns in the mirror and she knew it was the right one.

Sex for Elizabeth was still a matter of withholding – refusing to react, to be pleased or disappointed. She did this until Ross, the third or fourth time, stopped and said, 'Are you enjoying this? Or should we do something different?'

Elizabeth, unable to reply, watched as he put his face to her belly and kissed it, one hand sliding between her thighs. She twisted her fingers into the shorn curls of his dark hair and let her head fall back, prepared to wait patiently, to pretend. She looked out of Ross's window and saw the silver sabre of a new moon. She was taken completely by surprise to feel herself responding, her thighs letting go, flickers of pleasure running down from her stomach. She moved as if to free herself but Ross was insistent, holding her firmly until she came, grabbing at Ross's hair and gasping.

It had never happened before. Elizabeth lay still, appalled. Ross said, 'Are you okay?' and she opened her eyes to see him grinning at her, his eyes shining in the dark. She snatched her pillow over her face before she knew what she was doing, unable to look at him anymore. Then she felt him lie down beside her. He put one arm across her chest, and she felt the weight of it, heavy and warm.

The next morning she woke from a dreamless sleep to see Ross standing by the side of the bed and smiling down at her, haloed by sunlight. She held out her hand and he took it; she could feel the warm pads of his fingers against hers. It was a great relief to give herself completely to someone's eyes.

Ross introduced her to his friend Andy, who was a cook. He ran a café in Elizabeth's suburb. Ross and Elizabeth went there for coffee one afternoon and Andy came out from the kitchen in his filthy white trousers and t-shirt.

'This is Elizabeth,' said Ross, and Elizabeth had to make an effort not to lower her gaze, to look away while Andy frankly surveyed her. He waited a moment before putting his hand out, as though making a decision. When she took his hand he grinned at her. He had bright blue eyes and yellow hair that stuck up in dirty spikes. For a moment, Elizabeth wondered if Andy was someone she had slept with.

Andy did not have a girlfriend. A guitar leaned against the wall of his living room, behind the café. He still had some old records, stacked in a dusty pile beside a turntable. He switched the radio on as the three of them walked in. Later, passing it on her way to the bathroom, Elizabeth surreptitiously turned it down.

They sat on the floor and drank beer while Andy searched his kitchen drawers for drugs. Elizabeth and Ross held hands. Andy turned round, triumphant, brandishing a plastic sachet with a single tablet in it.

'Left over from last weekend,' he said, and shook the tablet into his hand. He used a knife, his deft, chef's fingers pressing on the black wooden handle to break the tablet into three. They washed the fragments down with beer.

Elizabeth thought it hadn't worked until she felt, quite suddenly, the hard warm fingering at the base of her skull. It made the hairs on her neck rise gently. She found herself pushing her bare foot back and forth on the carpet to feel its soft bristle, working up a gentle friction, making the skin on her calf stretch with pleasure. She listened to Ross and Andy speaking and felt like laughing at them. They looked so sweet under the lamplight. Andy seemed to glow.

Ross and Elizabeth drove home through the warm night without speaking. The traffic around them surged gently, a lapping tide of lights. When they reached Ross's house they fell onto the cool cotton slab of the bed. In her mind Elizabeth wandered and wandered. The pleasure of it was intense, and perfectly unfocused.

Elizabeth was late for a party; she ran down Ross's stairs, squealing with laughter, Ross chasing her. At the bottom he caught her and pulled her to him, pushing his face into her neck. 'Stay here,' he whispered, warm breath over her ear, 'please.' In the car her skin sang, and her mouth hurt from smiling.

They spent one last night at Elizabeth's place. It was after the slow leak of her possessions towards Ross's house had begun, before she had told Lucy that she was leaving. Her bedroom still had its desk and chair, but the wooden chest was half empty, its bottom drawer protruding like a sulky lower lip. There was a round mark on the carpet where the laundry basket had stood. She had not vacuumed for weeks.

They were woken in the early morning by the sound of a woman screaming through the wall. Ross was upright in a second, feet swinging round to the floor. Elizabeth sat up beside him.

They listened. The screams became wails and the wails terrible, painful sobs. They could hear a man now, his fast, nasty voice running under the woman's. Elizabeth and Ross were holding their breath.

The man paused and then said distinctly, 'Bullshit. Bull. Shit.'

The woman wailed again. The two of them were inside the house next door, their voices thickened by the wall, but Elizabeth and Ross heard footsteps; the loaded thump of the man as he strode out to their courtyard, the woman running barefoot behind him. Their voices became clear as they burst out into the morning air, almost directly below Elizabeth's window.

'It's always about money, isn't it?' The woman was crying. 'It's always about money with you.'

'It is where *you're* concerned,' said the man, his voice moving towards the back fence.

'If you loved me – if you loved me –' The woman was choking on tears.

'If *you* loved *me* –'

'I said I would pay you back. I'll give you the whole lot today. I'll ring Mum –' She became incoherent, but instead of talking over her the man was silent. Elizabeth and Ross looked at each other.

Then his voice became clearer again, as though he had stopped and turned around to face the woman. 'No,' he said. 'Fuck the money. That's it. We're finished.'

'Oh, no!' the woman shrieked, her voice rising and breaking. 'Don't!'

'Nup. I've had enough. Cancel Fiji, cancel everything.' He drew breath and delivered it, quick and cruel: 'I never want to see you again.'

The woman howled and choked. It sounded as though she was clutching him – or was she going down on her knees?

'Pack your bags,' he said. 'You can take whatever you want. Just pack your bags and go.'

Elizabeth and Ross remained where they were, listening, Ross on the edge of the bed with his feet on the floor, Elizabeth's hand resting on his arm. Their eyes met occasionally, but they said nothing. They had had several fights themselves; one that had seemed as though it could only end in separation. Ross had walked around his house with Elizabeth behind him, tugging at his arm, pleading, weeping uncontrollably. Now it seemed unimaginably distant.

The woman next door cried and cried and cried. Her voice swelled and faded. They heard her climbing the stairs of the terrace. They heard her dragging things around on the second floor.

The man stayed in the courtyard. Once, he shouted, 'I've changed my mind,' and Elizabeth and Ross gasped, staring at each other, but the man went on: 'you can't have the stereo. I paid for most of it. I'm keeping it.'

'I don't *want* the stereo!' the woman bawled, and again her crying became hysterical.

Later, long after the taxi had left, they heard him standing in the courtyard, talking on his phone. Elizabeth leaned out of her bedroom window to see him. The top of his head was balding. He was not wearing a shirt, and stood with his feet planted wide, one hand on a hip.

'I told her to pack her bags,' he was saying into the phone, 'so she did.'

'I could never leave you,' said Elizabeth, as they were driving back to Ross's house, 'but you could leave me.'

'I think you're wrong,' said Ross, turning into a stream of traffic.

'But what about –' Elizabeth was a little afraid to refer to it. 'What about that fight we had? I had to beg you to stay.' She looked out of the window.

'I wasn't going to leave,' said Ross. 'I was just angry.' He pulled up at a set of lights. 'But you could say nothing for years and then decide one day that you'd had enough. And never speak to me again.'

Elizabeth rather liked the sound of that. 'You think so?' she said.

Ross glanced at her. 'It's nothing to be proud of,' he said. 'It'd be better if you could tell me when you were angry.'

Caught out, Elizabeth could not look at him. She stared, eyes watering, at a car that was passing them, a car laden with a family and a dog. The dog had its head out the window, its mouth open, its tongue flailing backwards in the wind. She thought of Richard. They had never fought; when he'd disagreed with her and, later, the last time she saw him, she'd managed it by becoming still. She was doing it now, as she watched the family car pull ahead of them, surging forwards over the bridge. With the shock of confrontation came a quick cocoon, as though something had spun layers of silk over her. It filled her mouth, her eyes and ears.

Elizabeth kept her face turned away as Ross changed gears and they moved faster over the hump of the big bridge. She was not proud of the weeping and pleading but it was better than this silence. She tried to think of something to say, something that would sound cool and unconcerned. It would be a great effort to speak, to open her mouth and force words out.

At the bottom of the bridge they caught up with the family car. Elizabeth could have reached over and scratched the dog under the chin. It grinned at her, and a string of drool dropped from its tongue onto the road. A small dark-haired girl showed her head beside the dog's.

'Cute dog,' said Elizabeth, turning to face the road again.

'Yeah,' said Ross, accepting this offering.

As the months went on, Elizabeth began to see that Ross was not as gentle as he had seemed. He believed in honesty, he said, and if he thought that Elizabeth was bullshitting him he said so. When she told him she loved him he looked sideways at her and said, 'Don't just say it so I'll say it back.'

Now she could admit to herself that love was not quite what she had expected; a place where boundaries dissolved and difficulties disappeared, borne away on a tide of laughter. She could see now that love was chance, an invention, constructed on the foundations of sexual attraction and habit. She could see, too, that this was the first time she had been in love. She knew that she had never had any real intimacy with a man before she met Ross. He was so confident with her body, and with his own. He held her hand firmly, almost as a father does, when they crossed the road. She liked to sleep with her face in the back of his neck, breathing into his warm dry skin.

Elizabeth learned to start sex herself, to wake Ross in the middle of the night by stroking his stomach, or edging closer to him until the lengths of their bodies met, as though they were sealed together. She was awed by his lack of disgust. There was no part of her body that he did not seem to like. Sometimes he laughed when they were having sex. He stood talking to her while she sat on the toilet. And one night when she vomited after drinking too much with Ross and Andy, he sat by the bed with a bowl and stroked the sticky hair back from her face.

If Ross asked her about the other men she had slept with she was dismissive.

'What about the first time?' he said once, when they were eating a bowl of soup in Chinatown.

'What about it?' Elizabeth said, and put a piece of broccoli into her mouth.

Ross rolled his eyes. 'What was it *like*? Who was it *with*?'

Elizabeth chewed and said, 'I can't remember.'

Ross stared at her, his chopsticks poised. 'What do you mean, you can't remember?'

Elizabeth knew she had gone too far. She swallowed the salty broccoli and said, 'I mean, I remember who but I can't really remember the first time.'

'Bullshit,' said Ross. 'Everyone remembers the first time. I'll tell you mine if you tell me yours.'

'I really can't remember. It all sort of merges into one,' said Elizabeth, and bent her head over her bowl again. She was being ridiculous, she knew. And there was nothing to be ashamed of in her first experience with Richard in the park. But she could not help feeling embarrassed by how hard she had tried to enjoy it, despite the sight of her shorts dangling from her foot, and the broken leaves and stones prickling and pressing into her back. The way she had, tentatively, whispered Richard's name in his ear. And, of course, what had happened later.

Ross was still staring at her when she looked up from her bowl, her chopsticks laden with noodles. She met his eyes and he shrugged.

'Alright,' he said. 'But you don't need to be secretive with me.'

Elizabeth's family and Ross's could not have been more different, although they had both grown up in big houses, with money behind them. Where Elizabeth came from it was behaviour that really mattered, not thought. Where she came from if you wanted something you tried not to make it obvious. You hid your desire under a layer of politeness, keeping your solitary hours for resentment when you didn't, after all, get what you wanted. For the first months of their relationship Elizabeth kept giving way: where they went, who they saw, what they ate was Ross's choice. If Elizabeth did not say what she wanted, Ross did not press her, even when she fell into an offended silence.

Ross's parents had not known harmony, pretended or otherwise. Ross's father Allan had run the house with his temper and his fists until Ross's mother had at last found the courage to send him away, changing all of the locks and taking out a court order forbidding Allan to speak to them. And now Angela was dead, Allan was gone, and Ross was alone. After his parents' divorce, Angela had kept their house, which had been her family's since her childhood.

'He was a bastard,' said Ross, when Elizabeth asked about his father. 'His dad beat him up, so he beat us up. Mum's family hated him.'

'How did they meet?'

'I don't know. Dad's family lived out west. But Dad got a scholarship, so he must've met Mum at uni. She was doing law before they got married.'

'Didn't you ever ask about it?' said Elizabeth.

'We weren't really that kind of family.'

In Elizabeth's family, her parents had been gods, and the story of their courtship was one each sister had taken in, and tried unconsciously to emulate. But Ross did not seem to be emulating anyone. He was untouched, clean. Free of parents and siblings, and maintaining a comfortable distance from his friends, he moved through life alone and apparently happy. He always knew exactly what he wanted. No-one rang him on his birthday. He was even-tempered, calm and amused when Elizabeth had trouble with her parents, her friends, or one of her sisters. Sometimes – hardly ever – he became sad about his mother.

Angela had died a year or so before Elizabeth met Ross, leaving him the house near the river. Angela and her older sister Penny had grown up in the house, and caught the ferry from the wharf into their girls' school in the eastern suburbs. The house was as big as Elizabeth's childhood home had been, and five or ten times the size of the places she'd lived in since. It was too big for two people. Exploring when Ross was not at home, Elizabeth found rooms as different from each other as they could be. There was a red room like a heart or a womb, in which plush chairs were arranged at sociable angles, facing each other over a coffee table. She knew, without asking, that it was Angela who had made this arrangement of chairs. It was impossible to imagine Ross even considering which way the chairs might point.

Adjoining the red room, at the very edge of the house, was a small, dark, book-lined room with a cabinet whose glass face reflected hers. The library, Elizabeth named it to herself, thinking of a man in a leather chair, feet up, avoiding the hustle of a family. There was a long back room, which once had been a verandah, looking down past trees and other houses to the distant river. It swelled with light. And upstairs there were four bedrooms, each ready for a guest, though no-one ever stayed overnight.

There was a photograph of Angela on top of the cabinet in the library. She was wearing a pale blue dress, and had light brown hair, blurred with white, pulled back from her face. In the photograph she was kneeling under a tree, perhaps in a national park somewhere. The tree was enormous; its spreading branches were cut off by the edges of the photograph. Angela looked very small. The person holding the camera had not been sure if they were photographing Angela or the tree. It was not possible to tell whether she was smiling.

Sometimes, in a drawer or thrust to the back of a shelf, Elizabeth found things that were left over from Angela's last illness. An oxygen mask, its clear tube neatly coiled. A packet of syringes. A cotton dressing, backed with pale blue plastic.

In the final weeks of Angela's life she had refused to return to hospital for more treatment, preferring to be nursed at home by Ross. But Ross, ever more practical than his mother, had known he could not manage this alone. He had used Angela's credit card to buy a flight from London for Penny, her older sister. He told Elizabeth that he had hoped Penny would think of this for herself, being easily able to afford such a trip, but she hadn't, because her husband needed her at home.

'For what?' said Elizabeth. They were sitting in the garden, having a cup of tea. It had been raining; the trees above them glistened.

'I don't really know,' said Ross, taking a sip of tea. 'I don't think he's sick or anything.'

'Just needed someone to cook his dinner,' said Elizabeth. She tilted her head back to look at the dark undersides of the leaves.

'I suppose so,' said Ross. 'Or wipe his bum.'

Elizabeth sometimes thought, but did not say, that Angela had expected a lot from Ross. He had moved home to be with her when she was diagnosed. Elizabeth tried to imagine looking after her own parents. She couldn't. They were still looking after their children, helping her buy her secondhand car, providing a deposit on a house for her two sisters.

'What about Penny?' she said.

'I haven't spoken to her since Mum died,' said Ross.

'Why not? Did you have a fight when she was here?'

'No,' said Ross, smiling slightly, 'I just don't have anything to say to her.'

A leaf, unable any longer to carry its weight of water, tipped a long stream of rain down the back of Elizabeth's neck.

One day Elizabeth asked Ross whether he had thought of reconciliation with his father. He did not even stop what he was doing to say, 'Why would I do that?'

'Because –' Elizabeth paused. 'He's your father?'

He didn't look at her, reaching behind the stereo for the speaker wire. 'That doesn't mean shit,' he said.

Elizabeth, who had imagined herself beloved by a father-in-law, said, 'But what if we have children?'

Ross laughed, and sat back so that he could see her. The hair on his forearms was dusty. 'If we do,' he said, 'they'll be better off without him.'

It was autumn when Elizabeth moved in permanently with Ross. She told him that she had never lived with a man before. It felt a kind of failure, to have had no practice at what seemed like such an adult thing. They made the final trip from her house to his on a sparkling morning when the leaves were glittering silver and birds sailed on the last of the warm currents. The boot of Ross's car rattled as they drove over the speed bumps in her old street, Elizabeth's saucepans jolting and clanking together. Her bed, dismantled, was strapped to the roof. When they reached Ross's house they would carry it down to the capacious cellar at the bottom of the garden.

Ross's bed, which had been his parents', was impossible to take apart. It sat in the middle of the main bedroom like a ship at its final berth. It was high off the ground; Elizabeth could sit on it and swing her legs.

They unloaded the car at Ross's house and set off together to walk down to the river. Ross led them down a steep, winding road, and showed Elizabeth a leafy passageway between two tall sandstone houses.

'This is where I used to keep my boat,' he said, taking Elizabeth's hand.

Although the day had warmed, the corridor of

trees was still cool. There were mossy stones for steps; Elizabeth gripped Ross's hand as her heel slipped from under her. She could see a blue glimpse between the dark leaves.

They broke out, at the bottom of the corridor, into salty light. The river lay before them, and in the distance the concrete curve of the bridge. They could hear the cars sighing over its arch, but closer, the lap of water on stones, the leap and plop of a fish.

They held hands. The day was still. The sun was overhead, warming their necks and hair.

How lucky Elizabeth was. She kneeled on Ross's bed and looked out of the window, down onto the expanse of grass that fronted the house, the sandstone path, the little row of crabapple trees that were beginning to lose their leaves. The air was clear and still. Angela had gardened all day, he said, working her way slowly across the grass and around the trees, trowel in hand. Ross mowed the lawn, as he had always done, but left the flowerbeds and trees to themselves. One of Ross's neighbours walked past with her stout blue cattledog. She caught sight of Elizabeth at the window and lifted her hand to wave.

Six months or so after she moved in, on a brilliant spring morning, Elizabeth answered the phone in the little library. She had gone in to find a book to read and become caught on the carpeted floor by an old atlas. She was kneeling over the map of China, neck aching, when the phone rang.

It was Allan, Ross's father. His voice was deep and tired-sounding, but more Australian than she had imagined. Months of picturing him as the villain had left her with the sense that he might have a dark, rich voice: a voice with an accent.

'Ross isn't here,' said Elizabeth, sitting up and pressing one hand to the back of her neck. 'I could ask him to call you back. He's at work. Where are you ringing from?'

'I'm in Spain,' said Allan, then, quickly, 'Don't worry about it. Tell him I called. I'll ring back some other time.'

He hung up without saying anything more and Elizabeth stood up on stiff legs to put the phone back. She was breathless with surprise. She had never expected to hear Allan's voice.

Elizabeth looked around the room as if it might be changed, then reached out to straighten the photograph of Angela and the huge tree. She left the atlas open on the floor.

Elizabeth waited until Ross was home from work to tell him, until he was sitting at the bench in the kitchen with a beer in front of him. Then she said, as casually as she could, 'Oh, I meant to tell you. Your dad called.'

She looked up from the saucepan she was stirring, tenderly aware of his reaction.

'He called here?' said Ross.

Elizabeth nodded.

'He must have been looking for Mum.'

'Doesn't he know she's dead?'

'Well, I didn't tell him.' Ross took a long swallow of beer.

'Anyway, he was looking for you,' said Elizabeth. She brought the wooden spoon to her mouth to taste the sauce, slightly burning the end of her tongue.

'What an arsehole,' said Ross. 'Calling here. What did he want?'

'He didn't say. He's in Spain.' She glanced at him.

'Still?' said Ross, and took another swallow of beer.

'What's he doing there?' said Elizabeth.

'He had this – mistress. This Spanish woman. When Mum chucked him out he moved back there with her.'

'He didn't leave a number,' Elizabeth said.

Ross set his bottle down on the bench. 'We might turn the answering machine off for a week or so.'

Elizabeth looked back at her saucepan. 'Okay. Do you want cheese with this?'

Lying in bed, exchanging stories, Elizabeth learned that Ross's shoulder was not sore because of leaning over his work, but because his father had broken it by pushing him down the house's central staircase. They had been arguing on the landing between the flights, and Ross had told his father to fuck off. You were not allowed to be rude to Allan.

Ross's shoulder had broken as he fell against the stairs. It hurt so much that he could not keep his balance; clutching it, he slid the rest of the way on his back, tearing the ligament that held the shoulder together. His mother, coming down from the top floor to try to stop them fighting, had screamed for Allan to stop, and Allan had turned on her, shoving her so that she cracked her head against the plaster wall. It was not long after this that Angela, at last, forced Allan to leave.

Ross's description of his father made Elizabeth think of Richard. You were not allowed to be rude to Richard either. It was even worse to laugh at him. Once, as they walked down a long street together holding hands, he had said to her, 'You should obey me,' and she had laughed without thinking, it was so ridiculous, and turning to him, had seen his face harden, his jaw clenching. He let go of her hand. She had apologised instantly, sick with terror at his rigid face. He could punish her for days at a time, ignoring her when she said, *Are you okay? Did I do anything wrong?*, stepping back if she tried to kiss him, refusing to rise to her efforts at conversation.

Elizabeth wondered if Allan had been the same – like a horrible little boy grown up, loosing his rage on everyone, making the world run to his own monstrous and changeable rules. She had, she knew, fitted easily into Richard's idea of how the world must be, rushing to appease him, careful of his moods. She herself needed life to be quiet, safe; she needed people to be kind to each other. She would sacrifice almost anything in pursuit of this goal.

She asked Ross if he had been scared of Allan.

'When I was a kid,' he said. 'For a bit. Then I got sick of him. I got bored, and I didn't care, except when he hurt Mum.'

'What did you do when he broke your shoulder?'

'I went into the kitchen and rang the police while they kept fighting. I had to lean my arm against the wall to stop my shoulder slipping out. What a prick.'

Elizabeth stared up at the white ceiling of their bedroom, and pulled the sheet closer around her. Perhaps she should tell Ross about breaking up with Richard. Ross knew she'd had a nasty boyfriend, a bully whom she preferred not to talk about. Ross and Elizabeth treated Richard – and Claire, Ross's apparently mad ex-girlfriend – as part of a mutually embarrassing past. But now they had been together nearly a year, and it was clear that they would stay together, if they could. They were happy, and they loved each other. Ross never laughed when she confessed to something shameful; he always listened soberly, and sympathised.

But Elizabeth knew that she was unable to introduce the subject gracefully. And why did he need to know, anyway? She lay still, waiting for the image of Richard to pass, until Ross put a hand on her stomach. He made his fingers drift downwards, and she turned to him, letting him cover her mouth with his own.

Ross was not violent himself, despite the example of his father. He never hit Elizabeth. He never looked as if he was going to hit her. He did not start fights in pubs, or get out of his car at traffic lights to thump some idiot through his car window. He was very contained.

When she told her mother about Ross's childhood, her mother looked at her and said, 'Oh, darling.'

'I told you. It's fine.'

It was, however, hard to tell how Ross would react when they talked about his father. Sometimes he was laughingly dismissive of him. He called him a fascist bullyboy, and refused to be serious when Elizabeth was sympathetic with him about his childhood, or tried to identify with what she once stupidly, stupidly called his suffering.

'I'm not suffering, babe,' Ross said. They were sitting in a restaurant. Elizabeth had drunk too much red wine. She could feel tears pooling warmly in her eyes, making the candlelight blur. 'I wouldn't get too excited about it if I was you.'

At other times, as though they had not had these exchanges, Ross became savagely sensitive at the mention of Allan's name. Ross usually moved smoothly and quietly; he was a naturally silent person, given to long, thoughtful pauses before he answered questions. But on an inexplicably bad day, when his father was the subject of their talk, he began to shout and to move suddenly, uncarefully. Sometimes he hurt himself. Once, he had broken two bones, yelling and flinging his hand out as though he had found he was holding something disgusting. His knuckles had cracked against the white shine of the fridge. Later they swelled so much that they became formless, a faintly purple mass. He hadn't been able to use the hand for weeks.

Allan never called back – or perhaps he did, and the call was lost into the silence of the house. Elizabeth enjoyed having no answering machine. When she came home from work the day simply ended, dropping off into food, Ross and sleep.

Elizabeth wanted a child but did not know why, or what it was about a child that she wanted. Was it company? She had Ross for that. Some of her friends had had babies. She'd envied them most when they were pregnant; so solid and peaceful, with their hands over their bellies. So certain.

She suspected herself of wanting a child in order to find purpose. She didn't particularly like teaching, though the students made her laugh. Everything for them was so urgent. She could remember feeling that way, and so did not let them see her smile when they came to class tear-stained or sulky. *I couldn't do the essay. I had the most terrible week.*

The offices the city campus were perfectly positioned to net the flood of winter sunlight, and Elizabeth's desk, to make room for the woman she shared her office with, faced the window. Elizabeth sat with her eyes aching, her computer flicking to screen saver and her underarms beginning to sweat as she tried to plan her next class. The boredom she felt was a barrier to any constructive thought. Her body felt sick, and slow.

Sometimes she saw Ross striding past, at the head of a drifting row of students. If he was on his own and her office was otherwise empty he'd stop, filling the doorway, and smile at her. It was such a comfort to walk over and put her face against his chest. His clean, strong smell bringing a moment of privacy amongst so many strangers.

Before every class Elizabeth ducked into the bathroom on one of the quieter floors, usually the first, which the students only used as an exit. She'd stand in front of the mirror, breathlessly adjusting her hair, leaning in to examine her skin. Her hair was thick and coarse, cut in layers so that it didn't sit round her head like a loaf of bread, and her skin was olive-coloured – almost yellow, she had to admit, in some lights – and faintly furred. When she turned her face the slight blonde down caught the light. She had, since Ross, learned to see herself as attractive. The small breasts and skinny hips were boyish, sexy, rather than embarrassingly formless. She wore jeans to teach in; the heavy material on her legs made her feel sturdy and confident.

If someone came in while she was looking at herself, she quickly washed her hands and left. But still, that glimpse of her face and body in the mirror made it easier to talk to the students. That reassurance of self.

Elizabeth had one particular friend at work: Mira, who'd had babies herself. Three daughters. She was older than Elizabeth. The students loved her. Three days a week she travelled uncomplainingly in from the outer west of the city, where she and her husband owned a house on the border of a new development, the kind with a manufactured lake in the centre. The first time Elizabeth visited – a long train trip from town and a ride on a suburban bus without a muffler – she walked down to the lake with Tanja and Vesna, Mira's older daughters. They stood on its edges throwing bits of bark and sticks, trying to hit a single floating waterlily. It was midsummer and the sun beat down from a sky that offered no cloud, no variation in colour: just a wide scorch of blue.

'Sometimes there are ducks,' said Vesna, who was seven.

'Not today,' said Tanja.

'Too hot,' said Vesna.

The house was airconditioned; when the three of them stepped back in the relief was immediate, and Elizabeth gave way under it, collapsing onto a sofa in the living room. The sofa was flowered and crusted with old food. The newest thing in the room was a television, two metres wide and one metre high, squatting on its little mahogany stand.

'It's so hot out here!' said Elizabeth.

Mira was pouring Fanta into a row of plastic cups. 'I know,' she said, 'sometimes five degrees more than the city.' She nodded out at the expanse of sun-crisped grass in the backyard. 'I can't grow anything. It all dies.'

Tanja switched the tv on and Elizabeth got up, coming over to the kitchen bench. She took a long drink of Fanta. 'Have you thought about living closer in? Closer to uni?'

Mira didn't look at her; she was putting the Fanta back in the fridge. 'Scott's work is out here,' she said. She closed the fridge and turned round to Elizabeth. 'And what could we afford in the city, with three kids?'

When Elizabeth spoke to Mira about having a baby, she looked thoughtful. 'It's not something you can really plan for,' she said. 'I mean, you can buy a cot and stuff. But otherwise . . .'

Elizabeth said Ross wanted to try for a permanent position before they got pregnant.

'But it might take a long time for him to get on staff,' said Mira. She finished her cup of Fanta. 'And then, it might take a long time to get pregnant.'

Back at home, at Ross's house, Elizabeth idly followed the path his mother had worn through the garden, bending down to pull out weeds or to pick the dead heads from flowers. She wished she could work the house somehow, that the house was her job. She wanted to move through it, changing it, like a sculpture, or a painting.

Later, after she'd had her baby, she would realise that she had never been able to rationalise her need for one, and that it was pointless to try. Even when she had long, reasonable conversations with Ross about it, when they planned for the years to come, imagining when they would start 'trying' for a baby as so many of their friends had, the need would force itself up into her mind, making no sense of everything she had just said. Trying to push the need down was like trying to close the lid of a cardboard box on an angry cat.

'I think I'll get my hair cut short,' she said to Ross one morning, as they lay on a blanket in the garden, reading their books. This was after they had made up their minds. In a year they would 'try'.

'Newsflash,' said Ross, reaching out to tickle the back of her neck under her thick pigtails, 'you'll look like a boy.'

That year, as summer was starting, they spent a week with Andy, who had moved to Queensland. He was cooking at a restaurant in the hills north of the border, and living in a house that was the second on a farm of a thousand acres, sitting at the foot of dark hills on a paddock of dry white grass. It was as though the hills were a rising wave, a crest of green, and the grass was the stretch of beach at its foot.

Elizabeth was glad of her short hair. Each day was so hot that her skin hurt when she stepped outside. The grass crackled with insects. If she threw a stone into the centre of the paddock there was a great burst of grasshoppers, springing into the electric air like the dirt thrown up by a skidding car.

Andy had a brown kelpie that he had bought from the farmer who owned the property. She had never been on a road, but roamed across the paddocks and into the hills, sometimes on her own, sometimes with her mother, briefly freed from her duties with the cows. There were snakes as well as insects in the grass. When the dogs found a snake there would be yelping and barking that rang right across the sky. Elizabeth worried about them being bitten, but Andy, already more relaxed after six months in the north, said they could take care of themselves.

In the evenings, when Andy was working, it was cooler and they climbed the hill to watch the sunset. They toiled up along the cattle track, heads down, not looking to the top. The kelpie rushed and crashed around them, thrilled to have companions. They couldn't see her but they could hear her, pushing, forcing, crunching through the grass, until she'd appear right in front of them, mouth a red and white flare of teeth and tongue. Poised for half a second, a grinning snapshot of herself, and then she'd be off again, the bend and crumple of grass giving away her zigzag path.

At the bottom of the property there was a clear, still-flowing river. They swam every day, floating on their backs over the bed of slippery stones, looking through the eucalypts at the silver sky. The dog reached the water before they did; you could hear the rustle of lizards, slithering quickly out of her mad way as she ran. Then the clattering splash as she hit the water.

One night the wind was high and the palm tree at the back of Andy's house bent and swung. The walls of the house pumped in and out. If you stood inside with your hand against a wall you could feel it, as though the house had a large, slow, irregular heart-beat. Was it good for a house to be flexible, like the palm tree, swaying and giving way to the wind? Ross's house, made of brick, always stood firm against a southerly, not shifting, letting the wind rage uselessly around its solid corners. His verandah was solid, and glassed in. During summer they sat there to watch the southerly coming. They could see it approaching, see the distant river turn grey and then the trees around the house begin to shiver. The rain would hit the verandah windows in a sudden sweep, but the house stood still and firm.

In Andy's house the floorboards dipped under you as you crossed them and closed doors opened of their own accord when you walked by. Turning on the hot water made the pipes crack so that you could feel their movement wherever you stood.

When Andy came home from work they'd sit on the wide front steps, drinking beer and listening to the frogs. They sounded like a banjo band, a laconic, laidback gang, sitting on their rocks and twanging. You could stop them by hurling a beer can into the yard. There would be a breathless pause, as though the frogs were all looking nervously at each other, wondering what would happen next. Then one frog, braver than the others, would strike up its tune again and in a second all the others would follow. Some-times it was so loud that a remark beside you could not be heard. Ross, Andy and Elizabeth floated on the sea of noise, separate.

Andy's house was an hour or so from the town where Elizabeth had last seen Richard. On Andy's day off he suggested they go there, have a surf at the beach, a drink at the bowlo, fish and chips. Elizabeth was surprised to find how much she didn't want to do this.

'I might stay home,' she said, following Ross into their bedroom.

'Really?' said Ross, turning to look at her. The sun was already bright through the dusty windowpanes. 'Have you seen my swimmers?'

'They're on the verandah.'

'Is my towel there too? Why don't you want to come?'

Elizabeth followed Ross back out to the verandah, where he snatched his swimmers and towel from the wooden railing. 'I wouldn't mind some time on my own,' she said.

'They're still wet,' said Ross.

Elizabeth crossed her arms and looked at him.

'Okay, then. If you really want to stay. Seems a shame.'

'I'll read my book. Go for a swim in the river. You two might like being without me for a bit.'

'Yeah.' Ross reached an arm out and hugged her against his warm body. 'Maybe we'll score.'

Elizabeth watched them drive away, the young kelpie barking at her from the back seat. Treacherously, she wished that Ross was less straightforward. A more sophisticated man, one more given to the arts of dissimulation himself, would have noticed that

Elizabeth was hiding something. He would have asked questions. He would have dragged it out of her.

Elizabeth turned back to the house, listening to her feet on the speaking floorboards. It was not really important, anyway.

The men were drunk when they got home that evening; Andy more so than Ross, who had driven home. Still, Ross was uncharacteristically gregarious, leaping up the wooden steps to catch Elizabeth in his arms, saying, 'I missed you!'

Elizabeth had cooked, and they sat on the verandah again with bowls of pasta on their laps, glasses of wine beside them. It was Andy who started talking about sex, when Elizabeth asked him if he'd been seeing anyone.

'Just waitresses,' said Andy, putting his empty bowl down on the floor with a crash.

'What do you mean, *just* waitresses?' said Elizabeth, bristling, and Andy said, 'I mean women who are as bored as I am. Or boring,' he added.

'You should try spending more than one night with them,' said Ross.

The frogs were silent; there was rain building in the air.

'I've seen some interesting underwear,' said Andy, after a pause.

'Yeah?' said Ross.

'Oh yeah. And some techniques. Boy,' said Andy, shaking his head, 'some real techniques.'

'Like what?' said Ross.

'Oh, shut up,' said Elizabeth, hitting him lightly on the shoulder.

'I want to *know*,' said Ross.

'Why?' said Elizabeth. 'Let's talk about something else.'

'Don't be so boring,' said Ross. 'You might learn something.'

'Charming,' said Elizabeth.

'They've all been younger than me,' said Andy. 'They're not like women our age.'

'How do you mean?' said Ross.

Elizabeth took a sip of her wine. She felt a little drunk.

'I don't know. They're so – relaxed. They've been having sex since they were about fifteen, and they've all tried everything, all slept with other women, all had threesomes. They *use* me,' said Andy reflectively. Then added, 'It's kinda fun.'

'Our students are like that,' said Ross. 'They're so, sort of – *open*.'

Elizabeth nodded. 'They're always coming out. And being supportive of each other. And the boys wear dresses.'

Ross smiled. 'That's right. They're totally different. I was a virgin when I was eighteen.'

'I remember,' said Andy, and laughed.

Elizabeth and Ross took the New England Highway home, wanting a comfortable, uncrowded road after the bony menace of the Pacific Highway. There was coreopsis, dancing yellow suns, lining the road as far as Glen Innes. After that, white daisies, crisp and papery in the afternoon light. They stopped in a small town and found a pub where they could sleep for the night. Their room smelled of decades of smoke and roast dinners. The bed was like a bolster slung between two iron bars; it did not give when they fell on it. That night they would find it resisting them, pushing their bones up hard into their bodies.

There was nowhere to eat except the pub, so they drove west to an old, beautiful, wide-streeted cattle town. At seven o'clock on a weeknight it was empty of people and cars. The sky behind the buildings was turning the dusty pink of a galah. The shadows yawned across the main street.

The restaurant was called the Peach Blossom Café, serving Thai, Chinese, Malaysian, Indonesian, Australian. They drank a bottle of white wine and ate their way through four dishes, each of them adorned with a fried egg. When they came out the sky above them was dark, but the air was so long and clean and clear that they could still see a yellow paint stripe on the horizon, far distant, where the sun was setting on another town. Trees stood like little black statues against the yellow light.

A couple of weeks after they got home to Sydney they found out that Elizabeth was pregnant. It was undramatic. Her period had been erratic for months, so when she did not bleed on time it was not a surprise.

After a while she made an appointment with her doctor to see if there was a problem; she had been meaning to for ages. The doctor talked of vitamin B supplements and evening primrose, but also took some blood to make sure there was nothing seriously wrong.

Ross was marking essays in the library when the phone rang.

'I have some news,' said the doctor to Elizabeth.

Ross came out to see who was on the phone. Elizabeth, still listening to the doctor, pointed at her stomach and mouthed the words, 'I'm pregnant.'

'Glass is a liquid,' Ross said to Elizabeth when she asked why the view through the verandah windows was so blurry, as though the panes were always smeared with rain. 'It's all running down and collecting at the bottom.'

She didn't ever bother to check if he was right, as it was such a satisfying explanation, and it was true that around the bottom sill the glass was very thick and uneven. There was a large wooden table on the verandah where she sat in the mornings, alone, with a cup of tea. She'd look over the roofs and gardens to the river in the distance, and all the while the glass would be slowly, slowly trickling downwards.

Two of the houses that stood between Ross's and the river were owned by old women, both unmarried or widows – unless their husbands were inside, trapped in some near-permanent arrangement of television, bed and newspaper. The women were always up early. Elizabeth watched them emerge from their side doors to walk around their gardens looking at the plants, each describing the perfect half of a circle until they met at the wooden fence that divided them. The woman on the right was short and white-haired; she stood on a slab of sandstone to talk to her neighbour, who was taller and could lean her bony elbows on the top of the fence.

Now that Elizabeth was pregnant she woke every morning at five thirty-one, a perversely precise hour. Her mother came at six am one day, also unable to sleep, and stood leaning her eager face against the liquid glass, staring at the old women. 'Look,' she said, 'just like my mother. She checked her plants every morning.'

'You can see a lot of changes from day to day,' Elizabeth said.

Her mother nodded, her forehead making a slight squeak on the window.

A lovely privacy took hold of Elizabeth during her pregnancy. While teaching, she felt the baby turn and turn. A liquid writhing, a gurgle, a solid bubble of laughter. Everywhere she went, the baby went too. People began to seem distant to her; faces smiling, hands reaching to feel her belly. For the first time in her life she did not mind what people thought of her, or what they might say about her. At night she lay on her side with her belly against Ross's back. The baby kicked; he laughed to feel the little thuds on his skin, but at last whispered, 'Alright. Goodnight,' and Elizabeth turned away, taking the movement with her.

The birthing class was held in a small anteroom at the back of the hospital, at the end of a series of twisting corridors. The women sat with their legs wide apart, hands draped over their stomachs. They were swollen with life; by contrast, the men seemed frail and papery, as though there had been a terrible sucking or draining. They perched on their hospital chairs, looking as if a breeze could puff them away.

The midwife held up a plastic model of a pelvis in one hand and a baby doll in the other. She opened her mouth to speak and a man with thick spectacles said, 'My German shepherd had ten puppies. One of 'em got stuck coming out.'

The midwife nodded and said, 'That can happen with babies.' She brought her hands together, fitting the doll's head into the pelvis.

'So I've been at a birth,' said the man with the spectacles.

'Good, good,' said the midwife. 'For a normal birth the baby is head down.' She emphasised the last two words as she pushed the doll's head farther into the pelvis.

'My wife's mother had a hard time with her,' said the man.

'The head faces the front,' said the midwife, twisting the doll's neck.

'Twenty-seven hours,' said the man.

'And the –' the midwife stopped holding the pelvis and doll up and instead wedged them against her stomach, pushing the doll as hard as she could – 'the body should curl up –'

'And then she had to have a caesarean,' said the man.

The midwife gasped with effort. 'The head comes down with every contraction – just a second.' She turned the doll's head. 'Not like this, hang on –'

'But my dog didn't,' said the man.

The midwife was red in the face, forcing her fingers into the pelvis and around the doll's head, getting a grip on its face, and suddenly, with a rush, dragging it out. 'There!' she said. 'Only it won't be like that.'

The class stared at her. The man with the thick spectacles said, 'I helped her. So I've been at a birth.'

In the last months Elizabeth and Ross had awkward, utilitarian sex, shifting themselves and their pillows around in the bed, trying to find a position that made it possible. Elizabeth could feel herself retreating, however, becoming distracted, thinking of the baby and its movement inside her. Sometimes sex brought on strong contractions and she would have to lie carefully on her side, holding her hands flat on the underside of her belly, while Ross peered over the hill of her body, his anxious face making her smile.

Elizabeth finished working and retired to the house. She took long sleeps in the middle of the day, laying her head on the pillow and instantly disappearing into darkness. When she woke the day would have changed utterly, from the clean light of morning to the ageing yellow of afternoon. Her cheeks would be cold. Elizabeth held on to the railing as she walked down the stairs to the kitchen. She ate standing up, moving from fridge to cupboard, her hands and jaws working as she opened packets, cut slices, pulled out jars of jam and blocks of chocolate.

The slight incline up the sandstone path to the gate was almost too much for her. She stood panting by the jacaranda tree, one hand resting on its scooped trunk. She walked around the block, clockwise every day, stopping to look over fences into people's gardens or to smile at women who were pushing babies in prams. There were babies everywhere.

Then Elizabeth, huge, uncomfortable, unable to turn over in bed without pulling together all of her muscles – and groaning as she did so – was woken in the middle of the night by a sudden deep shove from the baby. At the same time she heard a small pop! and warm liquid gushed from between her legs.

'Ross! Wake up!' She managed to get herself onto her side, and then up on all fours. Ross was saying, 'What, what?'

'My waters have broken! Get a towel, get a towel!'

Ross was dithering, bumbling around the dark room, bumping into things. It was so uncharacteristic that Elizabeth felt like laughing, but a vast adrenaline rush was starting up her body, first hot then cold, and she was beginning to shiver. Ross pushed the towel up between her legs and she managed to reach behind herself and hold it in place.

'Get a pad. And some underpants. And switch the fucking light on!'

Ross switched the light on, and the room became a bright cave. He rummaged in her drawers and found some underpants, black ones that were too small, that she hadn't worn for months, and brought them to her. Then he ran to the bathroom. She could hear his feet thumping on the boards. Elizabeth gingerly moved to the edge of the bed, still clutching the towel, and sat there, trying to calm her breathing. The last weeks of pregnancy had been fraught with false starts; Elizabeth could not wait for the labour to begin. Now that something really was beginning, though, she was terrified. The shivering would not stop.

Ross reappeared with the pad, pulling it out of its wrapper with shaking hands. He peeled off the backing strip, and stuck the pad inexpertly into the fork of her pants, then bent down so Elizabeth could lean on him. Stepping into the pants was difficult, and some of the amniotic fluid dripped onto the floor.

'Are you okay?' said Ross, looking up at her. 'Does it hurt?'

'Not yet,' said Elizabeth. 'We'd better call the hospital.'

When the pains began they did not start slowly, as she had been told they would. It was as though something had seized her and was squeezing her, twisting her like a sponge. She lay on her side on the bed, gasping, one hand frantically clenching and unclenching. She stared at her hand as though it was separate from her; it opened and closed, opened and closed against the blue sheet. Ross had come back from making the phone call; he squatted beside her and put a hand on her shoulder but she couldn't speak until the pain had passed.

'How was that?' he said when she began to breathe normally again.

'Fucking *hell*,' said Elizabeth.

Within an hour the pains were three minutes apart and Elizabeth was on her knees in the bath, Ross pouring hot water over her back. If he spoke she snarled at him to shut up. The only way she could manage each contraction was to talk through it, focusing on her words as though they were pictures appearing in front of her. She said *oh god, oh god, oh god* and *please, please, please, please, please*. When a pain began to release its grip she looked up at Ross, hardly able to see him. 'Help me,' she said.

'I need to get you to the hospital,' he said.

Somehow, she did not know how, he managed to get her out of the bath. He kneeled in front of her and dried her with his big towel. She bent over him and gripped his hair and shirt when another pain came, and he tried to keep still, though she could feel him losing his balance on the tiles. He dressed her in her pyjamas and led her carefully to the front door, stopping when she grabbed his hand and gasped her way through another contraction. In the car she remembered the long, thoughtful talks they'd had about pain relief, and said, 'If I'm not nearly there by the time we get to the hospital I'm having an epidural.' Another pain began; through gritted teeth she hissed, *'And I'm not discussing it.'*

Ross just nodded, and drove faster.

At the hospital she needed to go to the toilet. The midwife showed her where it was and then stepped back, out of the way. She could feel them hovering in the corridor. She sat on the toilet as another pain came and she tried her best to endure it. She stared at the walls, at the white ceiling, at her feet shaking on the floor. Tears came to her eyes, but it was too awful for tears; she could not cry. She could not be helped. The bathroom was cold and bright and there was one small window, high up, out of reach.

But there was more, and worse, to come – the pain that came after the midwife examined her on the bed, and stepped back, taking her gloves off and saying, 'This baby's coming. I'm going to prep.'

Elizabeth got down off the bed just as the contraction was climbing. She moved towards Ross, who held his hands out to her, but she batted him away and kept moving forward, as though pursuing something behind him. She had seen tears in his eyes but could not care; she tried to cry again but her own tears would not come. As she reached the wall of the labour room and pressed her hands against it she heard herself saying, 'Please. Oh please', but that did not help either.

They got her over to the armchair in the corner of the room, and Ross sat down, holding his arms out again. She fell to her knees in front of him as another pain started, this one a forcing, pushing, exploding pain. She heard herself groan and scream simultaneously, and she rammed her head as hard as she could against Ross's chest. She could feel him bracing against her, his muscles quivering, but all she could do was push harder, up on her toes now. It felt as though she was going to burst. She knew the baby was coming but she could not think how it would happen. It was too big. She was *exploding*.

Then the pain climbed down and she was gasping, and wiping her sweating face all over Ross's t-shirt. She only had seconds for this; another pain rose and the midwife said, 'Push now,' and Elizabeth screamed as she pushed. It was not as though she was pushing something out; it was as though she was resisting the terrible force that was splitting her open. A burning, a splitting, and she heard the midwife say, 'The head's out!'

She started to cry, but the midwife said, 'Not there yet! Get ready!' as another pain came. Elizabeth went up on her toes again and forced herself against Ross as hard as she could; harder, harder, and she could feel him pushing back against her; and she felt a huge release and a slithering, the feel of soft limbs snaking out of her and heard the midwife say, 'It's a girl!'

Elizabeth fell back onto her knees and buried her head in Ross's lap. He was shaking with sobs, and now she cried properly herself, letting herself go utterly, awash with relief. They helped her down into a sitting position and put the baby in her lap, and Ross leaned over her, but she could hardly see the baby through her tears, and hardly hear anything but the sound of her own sobs and Ross's.

Later, when Ross had gone home to sleep and the baby lay in her tight roll in the bassinet next to the bed, Elizabeth tried to think about what had happened. Her mind felt as tender as her body. She tried to approach the feeling, but could not. She remembered being trapped in the hospital bathroom by pain; the awful loneliness of it, the sight of her cold toes moving frantically on the tiled floor, the fluorescent light making everything blue.

It was a horrible trick; that was what it felt like. She had been completely innocent, coming open and unprotected into this dreadful arena of pain. No-one had told her, really, what was going to happen. Nobody had explained what it was truly like. She had been utterly, utterly helpless.

Again she found herself crying, not for happiness this time, or for relief, but for sorrow. She understood now what it was to grow up. She could see her old self – a small girl who had been tricked into a terrifying game: a game whose rules were mad, whose results were uncertain, a game that involved a very intimate dance with the possibility of death. Elizabeth, having survived, could not help but feel something that was very like grief; grief for herself.

On Anna's third day Ross said, 'I wish Mum could see her.' He sat on the chair by Elizabeth's hospital bed and wept, unable to wipe away his tears or blow his nose. He just sat there, hands in his lap, weeping. Elizabeth heaved herself up in the bed, displacing dressings and icepacks, and shifted over so that she was sitting in front of him. She put a hand on the back of his neck and drew him towards her, then bent her face into his hair.

Elizabeth herself lay awake when he was gone and thought about Rita. In fact, at first she thought about Rita's mother. Or she tried to.

'Baby blues,' said the midwife cheerily when she came in to take her temperature and Elizabeth was sobbing. 'Always happens on the third day.'

Rita's funeral, the first Elizabeth had ever been to, was held on a sunny day in a church that was packed to the rafters. It actually did have rafters, Elizabeth noticed. She and her family were late, and had to stand crammed against a cold painted wall upstairs, at the back. The foolish mourning face of a sculpted Jesus leaned into view as she tried to see what was going on down the front, at the altar. The coffin made her draw a sudden breath: it was an insult, its corners rudely cutting into the air.

After Rita's funeral they went to the cemetery, a journey that Elizabeth, inexperienced and stupid with shock, had not thought to expect. The sky was blue, the trees rang with cicadas. There was jasmine somewhere. The mourners, following the priest, trooped past the trees. There was no shade where they were burying Rita. There was a row of new plots in the turned-up orange dirt. Heat struck the back of their heads and the green carpet that was draped into the open grave was so bright that it hurt the eyes, singing its colour in the intense sunlight. Surely someone was going to put a stop to this. There was a pile of dirt by Rita's grave, ready to be shovelled on top of her.

A week later, Elizabeth caught the school bus back to the cemetery. She was too shy to ask at the little stone office; instead, she followed the memory, seeing trees and mausoleums that she must have noticed on the day of the funeral. At last she found the Catholic section. There were three new graves on its edge, heaped with flowers that were bleeding colour in the heat. She didn't know which one was Rita's. There were no stones yet, or crosses with names on them.

She stood there, hands by her sides, looking down at the graves. She looked behind her, into the stand of eucalypts. There was no-one there. She could hear the traffic from the freeway. When her feet began to hurt she sat down on the ground and watched the black ants scurrying this way and that, avoiding the cataclysm of dirt and flowers. Such a great change was too large for them to notice. They ignored it, and went busily about, sometimes running over Elizabeth's shoes, or her fingers.

Now, lying in bed beside the breathing bundle that was Anna, Elizabeth did not know why Rita's mother had not run forward at the funeral and thrown herself into the grave. What people could endure was beyond believing.

Virginia and Charlotte, Elizabeth's sisters, came to see the baby, considerately leaving their own children at home with their mother. They did not stand awkwardly by the bed, as other visitors had done. Virginia went straight to the plastic bassinet and picked Anna up, her curly hair falling so that, for a moment, it concealed her. Elizabeth had been unable to leave Anna alone in the room, showering only when Ross was there, and sitting on the toilet with the baby in her arms. She kept her eyes on Virginia as she took a seat, curving Anna comfortably into the crook of her elbow.

Charlotte sat on the bed. She was wide-hipped from carrying her own son, who had been born several months earlier. Her face, still smooth and fine-featured, had that burnished, otherworldly look that extreme tiredness can bring. It was winter, and the sun was hanging low in the sky, pouring a silver light into the room.

'Hey,' said Charlotte into a comfortable silence, 'I saw Richard the other day.'

Elizabeth glanced at her. 'Richard McGrath?'

'Yeah. At Coles.'

Elizabeth waited to see how she would feel.

Virginia was leaning over Anna, singing softly to her.

'He's married, to this woman who looks about ten years older than him,' Charlotte continued. 'She's English.'

'Give me the baby,' said Elizabeth to Virginia.

'She was beautiful,' said Charlotte. 'They had three sons. They were beautiful too.'

Elizabeth received Anna into her arms, bending her head to kiss the baby's cheek. 'Lucky her,' said Elizabeth, not looking at Charlotte.

'Oh, I don't know,' said Charlotte. 'I always thought he was a creep.'

'Really?' said Elizabeth. She arranged Anna in her lap, pretending to be smoothing out the folds of her wrap. 'Why didn't you say so?'

'You told me never to mention his name again.'

'Did you tell him I was married?'

'You're not,' said Charlotte.

'You know what I mean,' said Elizabeth. Anna's mouth twitched in her sleep as though she was smiling.

'He didn't ask about you,' said Charlotte. 'We just talked about school and stuff. And you've always hated him so much. It felt wrong to bring you up.'

'Right,' said Elizabeth.

When her sisters left she sat propped up in the bed, staring at Anna. Anna was still fast in her new-born sleep, her arms hanging slightly by her sides, her mouth turned down a little. Elizabeth thought about Richard. How would she feel if Anna became involved with someone so nasty, someone who treated her so badly? She began to cry; slowly, tiredly. Some of her tears fell onto Anna's small, creased face.

Elizabeth said to Anna, 'If anyone dares, if anyone hurts you, I will kill them.'

Anna smiled again in her sleep, and Elizabeth began to see how much of herself she would give to this small girl, how effortless it would be to let her own life go for Anna's. Easy, thought Elizabeth. Like that. She held Anna up, cradling her little bottom with her hand, and felt how her legs dangled helplessly. She shifted her own aching body into a protecting curve.

It was a small hospital, and quiet, so that Elizabeth could hear the conversation of midwives in the corridors, and knew when the woman with the metal trolley of food was coming. The slight squeak of her trolley wheels, and the murmur as she ducked her head into each room, like a gentle bee pollinating a row of flowers.

Calm from crying, Elizabeth sat up against her heaped pillows and took the cover off the plate. The food looked as though someone had boiled it all day, but she fell on it, grateful, starving. The hospital was overheated. Now Elizabeth felt sleepy with happiness, warm with content, not minding the snagging stitches between her legs, the aching muscles, the weariness. Richard was nothing, a speck. He did not exist. The love that she had for Anna and for Ross eclipsed anything he had done.

After eating she picked Anna up, changed her

nappy, fed her, wrapped her, and laid her on the bed. They slept facing each other, and were rested when Ross arrived, straight after work.

It was a cold day when they brought Anna home from the hospital. Elizabeth sat in the back with one hand braced on the baby capsule. The car seemed to be going horribly fast; Elizabeth had to stop herself from gasping when they went around a corner. The low winter sun flashed against passing cars and shop windows.

'Turn the heater up,' she said to Ross.

'It's on full,' he said.

'I'm *freezing*,' said Elizabeth. Her teeth began to chatter.

It took a while to bring the big house up to the heat and sunny comfort of the hospital. Ross had kept it clean, but in a pragmatic, unthinking sort of way. Washed dishes stood in stacks by the sink, and there was a pile of Elizabeth's clean clothes, unfolded, unironed, on the bed in one of the spare rooms, like bodies sprawled on top of each other. Once she had Anna fed and settled – and this took forever, hours, even getting her to suck felt impossible – Elizabeth went from room to room switching on heaters. Ross was scandalised at the waste of electricity, but Elizabeth would not listen to him. They sat down for a cup of tea and from upstairs, in the baby's room, came a waking grizzle. Elizabeth looked at the clock. 'Fuck. Forty minutes.'

People often say that motherhood is a secret club; that no-one tells you, even when you are pregnant, exactly what is going to happen. That if they did tell you, no-one would do it. But Elizabeth knew now why she hadn't been told everything. It was simple: nobody had enough time. The change that bearing Anna wrought on her body and her mind was so complete that she could not afford to slow down and pay attention to it, let alone talk about it – as, for instance, she had done when she was pregnant. Her pregnancy had been peaceful, quiet; she had stood sideways, looking in the mirror at her beautiful curve. Her back hurt, but she rested. She had worked, but she still owned the evenings and the weekends. Her feet swelled; she put them up on a cushion as she watched tv. She had imagined being a mother, lovingly setting her baby down in its cot, to sleep and sleep.

In the weeks after Anna's birth Elizabeth's breasts leaked constantly, although perhaps leaked was not the right word. When Anna woke for a feed, Elizabeth was lying on sheets that were not simply damp. The sheets were wet; her pyjama shirt was wet; the mattress was wet and the blankets were wet. Her teeth chattered and her neck ached with shivering as Anna fed. She stamped her right foot to allay the shrieking pain in her scabbed nipple. While Anna sucked, the unused breast, if bared, spurted milk across the room. The milk hardened into cracking white patches on the carpet, the sheets, even the walls. If Anna pulled away from the nipple when she was feeding – and she often did, as the flow was so fast that it made her choke – the released nipple would send a stream of milk into her eyes so that she spluttered and shook her head and screamed.

Elizabeth's vagina, when it was healed, was like a little cave. If she sat a certain way and then stood, it let out air with an unmistakable noise that she was too tired to find embarrassing. Ross looked at it for her. 'It's like it's got a little false entrance,' he said, resting his hands on her open knees.

'Can you feel the difference, though?' she asked. 'When we have sex?'

'Oh yeah,' said Ross, running his hands down her legs. 'A bit. No big deal.'

Elizabeth sat up and reached out for him; she put her face into his sweet, dry neck.

'Want to give it a go?' said Ross.

As each of them made the slow, painful transformation into parents – it was glacial change, vast and cracking, but imperceptibly slow – Elizabeth saw new things in Ross. His generosity was, it seemed, boundless. When she cried after a long day with Anna he put an arm round her neck, kissed her and said, 'You have the hardest job. It will take time.' He cooked without being asked to and continued to clean the house, leaving trails of washing powder in the laundry and rings of oil on the kitchen bench – but he did it. Elizabeth let go of everything but Anna and herself.

Ross's generosity was sexual, too – he wanted them to start having sex again, but he said he wanted to wait until Elizabeth was ready. He was thoughtful and careful and forbearing with her. But Elizabeth found herself unable to deserve his loving patience. She did not have even the faintest stirrings of desire. Sex was like something from another life; now that her body was in service to someone else, it could not imagine itself into sex, could not soften into the idea of it.

Sometimes Elizabeth had sex with Ross because it seemed, quite simply, rude not to. But when she did she was appalled to find herself having little flashes, little images of Anna at her breast or naked on her sheets, as she and Ross moved around each other. Sometimes she even saw Richard's face. She didn't tell Ross about this, and thought, hopefully, that it would pass. She hoped, too, that he would not notice how passionately in love she was with someone else.

So much was new; so much that had always been there for her to see. The world was no longer opaque. Standing in line at the supermarket, her eyes aching in the bright fluorescent light, Elizabeth watched women filtering through the doors, plodding past the windows, and understood how many of them were exhausted. There was a whole underclass of tired parents, moving like ghosts through the crowds of the young, the healthy, the striding, the childless. The fair-haired woman pushing her pram along the street outside their house was not going for a walk for fun, Elizabeth realised. She was walking because her baby would not sleep. She was passing houses she had passed every day for weeks, without seeing them. She was keeping her eyes fixed on the tops of hills or on the wheels of the pram as they bumped over the pavement.

At last it was spring. Elizabeth came out of the supermarket, turning her head to feel the sun on her face and neck. She walked over to a tree in the middle of the square to look more closely at its new growth. Each twig finished in a furled explosion of green, like a tiny, frozen firework. She held one gently between finger and thumb. She was so tired that she was trembling. The twig, feeling it, quivered in her hand.

In the new semester, when Anna was seven months old, Elizabeth agreed to take on a day's teaching a week, on Fridays, when Ross had no classes and could stay home. The first time she stood up in front of the class she could feel sweat on her upper lip. Her mind felt like a room that someone had filled with water. Nothing stayed in place. It was all there, but it lurched and floated and swam. When she sat down, while the students busied themselves into discussion groups, everything continued to slosh about. What should she do next? She looked around at the faces in front of her. She smiled if someone caught her eye. She missed Anna's body, the smell of it, the hands in her hair and sweet breath in her face.

She met Mira for lunch, walking to the café on legs weak with triumph and relief. Mira was standing at the café counter; she smiled, and kissed Elizabeth when she reached her.

'The first time I came back to work I had to go to the toilets to throw up,' Mira said, taking her wallet out. 'Right in the middle of the class. I thought I'd never go back in.' She looked up and nodded as the man behind the counter said, 'Salt? Pepper?'

'Why is it so terrifying?' said Elizabeth.

'Did you want butter?' said the other, shorter man to Elizabeth.

'Yes, thanks,' said Elizabeth, smiling at him.

'Because for so long you've been thinking about just one thing. And you're so protected. Remember Jodi? She had to quit. She came back full-time when her little boy was three months old and had a total nervous breakdown, poor thing,' said Mira. As she handed the taller man her money, he grinned and said 'Ladies are always gossiping.'

Mira's and Elizabeth's eyes met momentarily.

'You wouldn't call it gossip if we were blokes,' said Elizabeth.

The man kept grinning.

'We're having a conversation about work,' said Mira.

'Oh, I'm not having a go at you,' said the man.

'We know that,' said Elizabeth, but the man continued, 'It's just all the ladies who come in here talk and talk and talk about the people they work with. Gossiping.'

'And what do you talk about?' said Elizabeth, but he had turned away to take a lasagne out of the microwave.

'Five dollars and thirty cents,' said the shorter man to Elizabeth, and she handed it over the counter in silence.

They took seats at a tall table at the back of the café. Mira picked up a sachet of sugar and flicked it between her fingers. 'You should've heard them before you got here,' she said. 'That tall guy was asking me if I wanted a long roll or a short roll in this really suggestive way. Then he said, "Long is better for eating".'

Elizabeth shook her head. 'That doesn't even make *sense*.'

Mira, mimicking her unconsciously, was shaking her head too. 'I know,' she said. 'I know.'

When Elizabeth got home, her breasts hurting with milk, she let herself quietly into the house, closing the door carefully behind her. She stood in the wide hallway, listening. Anna's wand – a silver, spangled stick that her grandmother had bought for her at the markets – was at the foot of the stairs. Cocking her head, Elizabeth could hear voices. She put her bag down soundlessly and tiptoed up the stairs, avoiding, from long experience, the lefthand side, which creaked.

Ross and Anna were in Anna's bedroom: Ross sat on the floor with Anna in his lap, his back to the door. They had a book open in front of them. Elizabeth stood at the door, watching. Anna's hair had grown longer, but taken on Ross's curl. It kicked upwards in a blonde peak like Tintin's. She could sit up now, but not crawl. She was delightfully fat.

Ross said, 'Up jumped the troll. And he said, *I want to eat you up!*'

Ross took the car to work. Elizabeth took Anna into town to catch the train to Mira's. Riding down the long escalators at the station, Anna in her arms, she was passed by a brisk young city worker in a grey suit, a woman whose way of life was now completely out of Elizabeth's reach. The young woman stopped, quite suddenly, about ten steps below her. Elizabeth looked at the back of her head, fair hair caught smoothly into a chignon. Then she became aware of an urgency behind her, and moved farther to one side as a young man in business shirtsleeves and tie came clattering past. He jerked to a stop when he reached the woman, clutching at the shiny black rail for balance. He put his hand on her arm. Instantly she brushed him off, turned away, and burst into tears. Elizabeth held Anna against her, feeling her curly hair tickle under her chin.

Elizabeth could not hear what they were saying, but it was clear that the young man had done something very, very wrong. The escalator finished suddenly; the young woman stepped off, and over to the westbound platform. The man followed her. He kept reaching out one hand to touch her arm and then snatching it back as if she was hot. Elizabeth carried Anna off the escalator. She followed them, but tried not to stand too close. They did not see her.

The train approached, its thunder filling the tunnel, and Anna leaned out of Elizabeth's arms to see. The young man pressed his palms together, fingers outstretched as if in the most desperate of prayers. He touched his lips with his hands and then reached out to the woman again. The woman looked down, pressing her thumb and third finger against her eyes, crying briefly; then she lifted her head and stepped onto the waiting train without looking back.

Elizabeth followed the young woman onto the train, drawing herself in as she passed the man. He stood holding his attitude of supplication. She tried not to stare at the woman where she stood, one hand bracing herself against a pole. The air around her was charged with sadness. Elizabeth stepped by her, carrying Anna up the stairs and into the upper section of the carriage, where they sat down next to a window.

When the young woman got off the train, at a sunny, flower-filled station, Elizabeth leaned her face on the window to see her walk purposefully along the platform. The woman was halted momentarily by the sound of her mobile phone; Elizabeth watched as she pulled it out of her leather bag, looked at the screen, and then switched it off, slipping it back into the bag. The train heaved out and, turning her head against the cold glass, Elizabeth saw the young woman disappear through the platform gates, her sleek, flaxen hair shining in the sunlight.

Elizabeth wondered what her life would have been like if she had been able to resist, to show how she felt in the way the young woman had. The young woman had given the man no quarter. She was not afraid that she might be doing the wrong thing in resisting him. She had shown him that he needed to be sorry, and he was sorry. Elizabeth, shaky, blurred, vulnerable in a way that had only increased since Anna's birth, was never certain of her rights. Should she be honest with Ross about her feelings? Should she tell him that she never wanted to have sex again, but that she wanted him to take care of her, love her, find her attractive and never sleep with another woman? It would be good, she thought, to be so clear, and clearly understood.

They'd had sex the night before and Ross's creaking old bed, or something else, or nothing, had woken Anna, just after Ross had come. Elizabeth tried to wriggle out from under him, but Ross, now a soft, warm weight on top of her, was hard to shift.

'What are you doing?' he said.

'I'll just settle her,' said Elizabeth.

Anna wailed and she wriggled again. Ross rolled off her, and she sat up.

'She can wait,' said Ross.

'It won't take a sec,' said Elizabeth, swinging her legs around.

'But I was going to go down on you!' said Ross.

'Okay. I'll be back in a sec.'

But as it turned out, Anna could not be settled

easily, and Elizabeth had to breastfeed her, her nipples still tender from Ross's touch. She wondered if the chlorine smell of sperm would disturb Anna, would intervene in their closeness.

When Anna was finally asleep in her cot, Elizabeth tiptoed back down the hall to their bedroom. Ross was asleep too, his back turned to her. Elizabeth felt herself relax. She slipped into bed beside him and put one arm over his broad, sweet back. He murmured, 'Do you want something?' and she whispered, 'No,' into his skin, and closed her eyes.

At Mira's house her youngest daughter, Lily, was mixing water and flour with hundreds and thousands.

'She's making a cake,' said Mira, as they sat down at the table.

Lily grinned and looked up, bringing her wooden spoon out of the mixture and flicking a dollop across the room. It landed on the back of the couch.

'Oh, sweetie,' said Mira, without moving, 'be careful.'

Anna leaned back in Elizabeth's arms, reaching around the back of her head for her hair. A wedge of sunlight passed through the windows.

Tanja and Vesna came home from school, streaming into the kitchen, shedding bags and jumpers and hats. They swarmed over the breadbin and the fridge. Elizabeth looked at their beautiful bony brown legs, at their thick white socks. Food in both hands, having barely stopped to say hello to their mother, and without acknowledging Elizabeth at all, they went outside, into Mira's vast back garden. The dog, which had lain silently in the shade of the garden furniture all day, sprang to its feet and rushed at them, leaping and barking joyfully.

Later, Tanja came in to watch television with Lily. Lily's cake was cooking in the oven, giving off a faint, bready smell. She sat with her thumb in her mouth, absorbed, not hearing when Elizabeth said goodbye. Tanja turned and smiled and was quickly snatched back by the tv. Elizabeth was standing at the kitchen table, a sleepy Anna leaning over her shoulder, when Vesna shouted from the backyard, 'Mu-um!'

'Just a minute, Ves! I'm seeing Elizabeth off,' called Mira, pushing her chair in. She smiled at Elizabeth. Through the window they could see Vesna tying her skipping rope to the fence. She was concentrating on the knot she was making. Without looking up she called, 'Mu-um! Do you love me?'

'Hang on!' shouted Mira. And then to Elizabeth, 'Sorry. Can I kiss Anna?'

'Of course.' Elizabeth held Anna towards her, and Vesna bawled, 'MUM! DO – YOU – LOVE – ME?'

'YES!' bawled Mira suddenly, and Anna jerked back in Elizabeth's arms, eyes wide open.

'Sorry!' Mira blushed.

Elizabeth laughed, and from the garden, finishing her knot and tugging at it in a satisfied way, Vesna screeched, 'GOOD!'

The letter from Ross's father came on a day when they'd had a fight and Ross was lying on their bed with his hands folded behind his head, watching the ceiling. Elizabeth took Anna out to the letterbox with her. She could be an awkward child to carry, preferring not to sit up in your arms; instead, she leaned forward from the waist, staring upside down at the ground, like a monkey in a tree. But Elizabeth showed her the letter with the Spanish stamps on it and she came upright immediately, fingers reaching.

Back inside, Elizabeth climbed the stairs and put Anna down on the bed next to Ross, with the letter in her hands. Anna was making little gasping noises, jerking the envelope as though she was trying to open it but had forgotten how.

'What's this, darling?' Ross said to Anna as Elizabeth retreated. 'What have you got for me?'

Elizabeth was making a cup of tea in the kitchen when a change in the light made her look up to see Ross standing in the doorway, Anna in his arms. He freed one hand, pulled the crumpled letter out of his back pocket and passed it to her.

'What's he got to say?' said Elizabeth, taking it. 'Sorry?'

Later, before they sat down to dinner, Ross said, 'We're not going. So don't try and make me.'

Elizabeth held up her hands, palms facing him, saying nothing. Anna squawked from upstairs.

'Why should we?' said Ross.

'Are you going to settle her or will I?' said Elizabeth.

'You,' said Ross, but he followed her up the stairs to the bedroom and stood outside as she gave Anna her dummy.

'He doesn't deserve it,' he whispered as she came out, pulling the door to behind her. 'He's an arsehole.'

'It's up to you,' said Elizabeth, putting a finger over her lips.

'Don't say that!' said Ross. Elizabeth edged to one side and slipped past him, padding quickly down the stairs towards the kitchen.

The morning after the letter arrived they put Anna in her pram and went for a walk down to the wharf. Ross's suburb – Elizabeth still thought of it as that – was the kind where the streets became busy from seven am. The yellow newsagent's van, an arm curving out of it to send the rolled papers to thump! in the green centre of walled gardens. The men and women in their sixties, walking border collies and spaniels. The young women in tiny shorts and sneakers, headphones on as they sped silently past. And schoolchildren in ties and boaters and uniforms with dropped waists, stripes, and long socks, shouldering their way to the bus stops, little mules under their burden of books.

They pushed the pram to the end of the wharf. It was high tide and the water was as still and dark as oil. Ross bent down to pick Anna up, pulling her blanket around her, holding her so that she could see out towards the city, where scalloped yellow clouds made way for the sun.

'What if he's lying?' said Ross.

Elizabeth reached out to straighten Anna's blanket, making Ross jerk back in annoyance. 'What about?' she said, putting her hands apologetically behind her back.

'What if he hasn't got cancer?'

'It's a big thing to lie about.'

'That wouldn't bother him.'

Elizabeth was not really listening to Ross, concentrating instead on not interfering with the way he was holding Anna. Her whole body wanted to reach towards the baby, snatch her from her father, whose breath was beginning to shorten, who was beginning to move agitatedly about on the greying planks of the wharf.

'Why would he lie? He could just ask to see us. Wouldn't we go, if he asked?'

'I wouldn't piss on him if he was on fire!' said Ross, and Anna twisted her head around to look up into his face. A ferry disappeared into the next bay just as its ripples arrived at the wharf, making the dark, heavy water lap against the pylons.

'Okay. Okay, then,' said Elizabeth, and put a hand on his arm as he stepped backwards to the edge of the wharf. 'We won't go.'

'That's easy for you to say!' cried Ross, and Elizabeth, unable to prevent herself, caught hold of his t-shirt, pulling him forward and then taking Anna from his arms. She held Anna against her breasts.

The second letter came six weeks later, after the first went unanswered. It had a cheque in it, enough to cover airfares, hotels, the hire of a car. Allan's house was big enough to take them all. He had a nurse living with him, he said. They would not have to help him. His house was one of several on a farm in the mountains. There was a stream, there were sheep, pigs, a pond with ducks and geese in it.

'What does he think, I'm going to play with the ducks?' said Ross, holding the letter in one hand and the cheque in the other.

'It would be nice for Anna,' said Elizabeth.

Ross was re-reading the letter. 'He doesn't even know she exists,' he said, not looking up.

Elizabeth was washing up. Ross stood in the kitchen watching her, his back against the bench. He was drinking a glass of wine.

'Careful!' he said, as Elizabeth crashed a plate into the sink.

'I thought you said they were unbreakable.' She pulled the plate out, dripping water, and put it into the metal rack.

There was a pause.

'I did,' said Ross. 'But I don't want you to scratch them.'

Elizabeth turned round to face him, another plate in her hand. 'You're kidding, aren't you?'

Ross looked straight at her. 'They are unbreakable,' he said, 'but they aren't – unscratchable.'

Elizabeth held the plate up. 'They're covered in scratches already.'

'I don't want you to scratch them more!'

'Ross –' said Elizabeth, 'they're old, crappy plates. They break and they scratch and you've never given a shit about them before. You just haven't got the guts to say you're angry!'

'They're unbreakable,' said Ross, putting his wine down and taking the plate from her. He held it above the tiled floor. 'Look –'

'Don't!' said Elizabeth as he let go. The plate crashed to the floor, smashing into stars of glass. Their eyes met; there was a silence. Then, the rising cry from Anna's bedroom.

'Who's going to settle her?' said Elizabeth.

'You,' said Ross.

'How about you do it?' said Elizabeth.

'You're better at it,' said Ross.

Elizabeth nodded, and left the room. She ran lightly up the stairs. By the time she got to Anna's room Anna had stopped crying. Elizabeth stood in the corridor, listening, feeling her heart beating. She put one hand against the painted wall and looked at her fingers, red from washing up. Downstairs she could hear Ross sweeping up the broken plate.

They lay in bed that night, listening to the distant river. They could hear a ferry cruise passing – music, the chug and wash of its progress and, surprisingly, the drunken talk of revellers as they hung over its rails. During the day you could not hear anything from the river; it was all masked by the daily sounds of cars and dogs and people. Even the boats crawling noiselessly but surely across the blue could not change the impression that the river was a postcard, that it could be peeled away quite easily, leaving nothing but a soaring space behind it.

At night, however, it was as though the river was alive, and whispering to itself, right outside their window. As though, if they leaned out, they could trail a hand in its dark water.

Ross moved so that the length of his body was against Elizabeth's. He was warm. He curled his foot over her leg.

'We'll go if you want,' he whispered.

He always waited until the lights were off to tell her important things. She turned to look at him; could just make out his eyes and the shape of his nose. 'Do you think so?' she said.

'I want Anna to see him.'

'Okay,' said Elizabeth.

He shifted closer, so that his thigh was on top of hers. The hairs on his leg made their slight rustle against her. 'I don't care if he sees her. I'll do it for Anna, but not for him. And I'm not rushing, okay? I'm not taking the next plane to get to his fucking deathbed. If he really is dying.'

The next day, after they had put Anna down for her nap, Elizabeth said, 'Do you think we should go to England as well?'

'What for?' said Ross.

'To visit your aunt.'

They were sitting in the red room, in that sudden drop of energy that came once the baby was in bed.

'It hadn't occurred to me,' said Ross. He was silent for a moment. 'I don't know if you'll like her.'

'She might like to meet Anna. We won't get another chance like this,' said Elizabeth, shifting around on the cushions. Her back was sore.

'I suppose so,' said Ross. 'Let me have a think about it.'

Later that night, again in bed, after the lights were out, Elizabeth whispered, 'Why wouldn't I like Penny?'

Ross turned over so that he was facing her.

'She's a bit like my mum,' he said.

Elizabeth waited. She could smell toothpaste, and the warm scent of Ross's body as he moved in the bed.

'Sort of – a bit sad.'

'You mean hopeless? Or just – miserable?'

'A bit of both. And kind of fussy and uptight.'

'Maybe her husband beats her,' said Elizabeth without thinking, and then sucked in her breath quickly, saying, 'Sorry!'

She could see Ross's teeth as he grinned. 'Don't worry about it,' he said. He touched Elizabeth's face and ran his fingers down her neck. 'I don't think he's the beating type.' He paused. 'Do you feel like a fuck?'

Elizabeth sighed. 'Not really. Sorry.'

Ross let his fingers drift down to her breast and

brush against her nipple. 'Are you sure?' he whispered.

'Yes.'

His hand was on her stomach now; Elizabeth put her own hand over it and said, 'I really don't want to.'

'You never want to these days.' Ross was still trying to stroke her stomach.

'I do! We did it just the other day!' She pushed his hand away, and Ross snorted, turning on his side.

'Three weeks ago,' he said. 'You're no fun.'

'I am,' said Elizabeth, looking down towards her feet. 'Just not this second.'

It was not easy, this continual deferring of the moment. Was she lazy, Elizabeth wondered. Or was there something really wrong? She put a hand up to her breasts. They felt like flaps of fat and nothing else, dry and rubbery, not very warm, attached to her body but meaning nothing. Only when Anna was breast-feeding did they begin to change; the tingling, the fingering of feeling that started in each breast as the milk came down.

The next day at work Ross made a phone call to a travel agent to book their tickets. When he came home he told Elizabeth that he had been able to get a cheap extra flight to Madrid from London. 'So we'll fly to England first, then to Spain. We'll take our time.'

'What about your dad?' said Elizabeth.

'He can wait.'

'Okay,' said Elizabeth, nodding. So far she had not had to do a thing.

Charlotte and her husband came over for dinner before they left. They sat at the table on the verandah with the ruins of a meal around them.

'So what's he like, your dad?' said Charlotte, reaching out to pick an olive from the wilting salad.

'I already told you,' said Ross. 'A wife-beating drunk.'

They laughed.

'So why are you going to see him?'

Elizabeth looked at Charlotte, who was spitting the pit of her olive into her hand.

'He's dying,' said Ross.

'Yeah, but you don't like him,' said Charlotte, and laid the olive pit on the side of her plate. Her husband made a mild sound of protest.

'I know. I just want to make sure he really does die.'

They laughed again, and Elizabeth said, thoughtfully, 'Maybe you want to – sort of – have it out with him.'

Ross made a face. 'Doubt it!'

On the morning of the day they were due to leave, Elizabeth and Ross lay in bed listening to Anna wake up. At eleven months she no longer woke with a scream of rage or hunger – now she swam up out of sleep on little currents of chatter and laughter, eventually surfacing on a word that sounded like 'Mu-um!'

Elizabeth sat up so that she could see out of the window: the light playing on leaves as a breeze nosed through them; in the distance, the blue river. She listened to the quiet, hoping to absorb it, store it for the journey.

Ross took her hand. Elizabeth looked down at him. 'I should get up,' she said.

'I just wanted to say something,' said Ross, and Elizabeth said, 'Uh-huh,' swinging her legs round to the side of the bed.

Ross looked at her.

'What?' she said.

'I'm trying to be intimate,' said Ross, frowning.

'Sorry,' said Elizabeth, and tried to look attentive.

'I just thought that our holiday would be a good chance to – you know – to start having fun again.'

Elizabeth was puzzled. 'You mean – like going out?'

'I mean sex,' said Ross. 'I mean we could start having more fun with it. You could relax a bit.'

'Right,' said Elizabeth, feeling herself shrivel, like a snail into its shell.

'I'd like us to have sex more often. And to enjoy it more.' Ross paused. 'Don't you think?'

'Yes,' said Elizabeth quickly, 'I think you're right.'

From her bedroom Anna called, 'Mu-um!'

Elizabeth tried to pull her hand out of Ross's but he kept hold of it. 'I really want you to think about this,' he said.

'I will,' said Elizabeth. 'I promise I will.' She slipped her hand away and was out the door before he could say anything more.

*

Their flight from Sydney was a late one, at a time when most flights were arrivals. After checking in they walked along the quiet carpets of international departures, Elizabeth carrying a sleeping Anna.

'Is that someone lying down?' said Ross as they passed the last gate.

He was right; there was a figure on the carpet, in the shadows ahead of them. As they got closer they could see it was a man. He had his bag beside him. He was lying flat, arms by his sides, eyes closed, corpse-like. The lights were being turned off. Behind them, in the distance, people were pouring out the doors, emptying the airport like an hourglass.

They reached the man and stood over him. He was completely still. His nose was bloodied; there was a smudge of blood on his dirty, pale jeans, and a drip of flesh protruding from his cheek, as though a cat had caught its claw there and pulled the soft inside out.

'Excuse me.' Ross bent down and laid a hand on the man's arm.

The man's eyes jumped open; he stared up at them, his body still.

'Are you okay?' said Ross.

'Where am I?' said the man. 'Have I got money?'

Elizabeth saw his wallet on the floor beside him, sprung open by a wad of twenty dollar notes. She shifted Anna onto her shoulder, squatted, and showed it to him. 'You've got plenty,' she said.

'Where am I?' said the man again. He blinked his red-rimmed eyes.

Ross held out a hand to him, which he took, pulling himself with difficulty to a sitting position. Elizabeth stood up.

'You're in Sydney,' said Ross. 'At the airport.'

The man, now getting to his feet, had no balance; he swayed weightlessly. 'I'm supposed to be in Singapore,' he said.

Elizabeth was holding the man's wallet while Ross steadied him. She glanced down and saw, behind a square of greasy plastic, a photograph of a woman and two children, a boy and a girl. Their smiles were studio smiles. The woman's hair was combed out and fluffed for the photograph.

'Do you want this?' Elizabeth tried to hand him the wallet.

The man looked at it, head nodding on his neck as though on a loose spring. 'I've got money,' he said, and then looked up at Elizabeth. 'I,' he said, 'am the drunkest man in Australia.'

'Are you,' said Elizabeth, and glanced at Ross.

They walked the length of the carpet with him, Ross carrying his bag and steadying him with one arm, Elizabeth still holding the fat wallet. Anna's head lay heavily against her breasts. The airport was empty now, except for the clot of people around their departure gate. Elizabeth left their little procession there, pushing the man's wallet into his bag and sitting down on one of the seats in the padded row. She watched as Ross led him up to the security guards at the entrance, guiding him as his legs wove their way across the patterned carpet. Anna dribbled warmly down the bare skin of her neck.

'Poor guy,' said Ross, as they stood in line to get on the plane.

'You think so?' said Elizabeth. The stewardess gave them a professionally indulgent smile, tilting her head to look into Anna's sleeping face as they handed over their boarding passes.

'He must be pretty miserable, to get that shitfaced,' said Ross. 'Anything could have happened to him.'

'I didn't like him,' said Elizabeth, and Ross laughed. 'I'm not asking you to like him.'

But Elizabeth shook her head.

Anna continued to sleep on the plane, in the pull-out bassinet attached to the wall in front of them. The plane was dark now, and people sat in little pools of light, nursing drinks or reading, or staring at the seat in front of them. Elizabeth and Ross didn't speak, but couldn't sleep, listening to the scream of the engines. On take-off Elizabeth had felt, and resisted, a surge of panic: the sure knowledge that if something was to happen she would be unable to protect Anna. She prevented herself from thinking about the endless metres of air below them, about the hard metal of the oceans. If she suspended disbelief the plane would stay aloft. She stared across the aisle at the rows of helpless people, strapped in.

There was a man in the outside seat with dark blond hair and brown skin. He turned and smiled as he felt Elizabeth looking at him, and for the briefest of moments she thought he was Richard. She turned away without smiling back, aware of being rude, her heart bumping.

Since she and Ross had made up their minds to go, Richard had reappeared in her dreams. He did this every year or two, when the skin of her life was stretched thin over her unconscious. The dreams were always the same. She met Richard at a party and he talked to her intensely, intently. He kissed her. She was about to go off with him, very excited, when she remembered Ross. Regretfully, she had to turn Richard down. He was so attractive, but not worth the risk.

Elizabeth knew herself to be a liar, in her dreams as in her waking life. She knew that she was not going to try to relax into more sex. She knew that she loved Ross, and wished that everything could be solved between them. He could not be compared to Richard, with his Norman Mailer book and his crude, selfish demands. But nonetheless every sexual encounter was beginning to feel like an invasion; Ross's confident, moving hand felt like the scout for a whole skirmish of violation that was to follow. In those moments it was hard to believe that Ross meant well; how could he, advancing on her body like that?

It was stupid. Elizabeth moved her shoulders irritably, bumping Ross. He leaned over and kissed her neck. His face smelt of baby wipes; he must have used one to cool himself down. 'I'm so glad we're having this holiday together,' he whispered, 'we'll have a great time.'

Elizabeth, ashamed, turned to look at her shadowy reflection in the window.

Unlike Sydney, Heathrow was clotted with security guards, staring about them, speaking into walkie-talkies. Two of them watched dispassionately while Elizabeth settled herself on a bench and began to breastfeed Anna. Anna smelled of sweat and shit, as did Elizabeth. Ross, standing by the bench and scanning the crowd for Penny, smelt only of sweat.

Eventually Penny appeared through the people, a pale, thin creature in a long ugly dress. Her hair was fair and greying. She smiled uncertainly when she saw Ross. They did not kiss, but Penny bent down to Elizabeth, and their cheeks touched. She had sixty year old skin that had hardly seen the Australian sun in decades and was silky, even furry as they brushed against each other. Elizabeth could smell shampoo and a blossomy perfume. Penny spoke gently, so that it was difficult to hear her in the rush of the airport. She had rather prominent teeth, and an English accent. Her large, faded blue eyes, like cornflowers left in a vase by a window, filled with tears when Anna was held out to her.

She and her husband Geoffrey lived in Richmond, near the river, in a big house with a conservatory at the back. Geoffrey met them at the door. He was as pale as Penny, with an attenuated look and a clipped, toneless voice. He greeted them without smiling, or looking at Anna, and led them straight up the stairs to their rooms, explaining the plumbing and the heating as he went. Elizabeth was desperate to go to the toilet, and to wash herself and Anna, but could not disengage herself from Geoffrey, who stood by the bathroom door, saying, 'We had a new boiler put in last week. You'll find the water very hot when it comes out.' Elizabeth could hear Anna, who was being undressed by Ross in the bedroom, screaming with exhaustion and rage.

At dinner Geoffrey was generous with his wine, rising from the table two or three times to find another bottle in the fridge or the cellar, asking them to choose which they liked best. He brought out Australian shiraz, New Zealand sauvignon blanc, South African chardonnay.

Elizabeth picked up the bottle of sauvignon blanc.

'Can we have this?' she asked Geoffrey. She held it out to him, and he took it, and looked at the label.

'Funny how so many wines have got screw caps these days,' said Ross.

'The correct term is actually Stelvin cap,' said Geoffrey, twisting it off with a slight crack.

'Uh-huh,' said Ross, holding out his glass.

'It's amazing how many people won't buy a wine that has a Stelvin cap on it. In fact the Stelvin cap works better than a cork. Wine never goes off with one of these, and you can reseal it so easily.'

'Yes, it's much more convenient, isn't it,' said Elizabeth politely, accepting a large glass from Geoffrey.

'People think that if a wine doesn't have a cork then it's somehow not the real thing. All they need to do is taste a bottle of wine that's been "corked". We did once, remember?' He turned to Penny. 'In Provence.'

'That's right,' said Penny, nodding.

'I sent it back,' said Geoffrey. 'They wouldn't believe me at first. I had to be firm. I said to them *This wine is corked*. Then I said it in French. *Ce vin est bouché*. Do you remember?'

Penny had begun clearing the dinner plates, though she had not yet stood up. 'I do remember,' she said, not looking at Geoffrey. Elizabeth and Ross met each other's eyes across the table.

He went on and on, murdering every subject, until Elizabeth wanted to scream, to jump up from the table and run around shrieking as if her hair was on fire, every time he spoke. She stared at him, trying not to listen, until he had a silvery outline and all his words ran together. When Penny talked, her small remarks about weather and the dearth of fresh fruit at the supermarket were like spring rain after the deadening snow of Geoffrey's conversation.

'I'm going to kill him,' whispered Ross when they were in bed, listening to the sounds of Penny and Geoffrey getting ready for sleep: the rattle of a curtain, the discreet flush of the toilet.

'If I don't kill him first,' said Elizabeth.

They lay in bed, unable to sleep, their legs entwined. Elizabeth's ears sang with the distant roar of the plane.

*

When Elizabeth came down with Anna in the very early hours of the morning, the table, which last night had been covered with dinner plates and wine bottles, had been cleared and set for breakfast. There were four plates, four bowls, four smaller plates, all of smooth white porcelain; four glasses, four teacups on saucers, four silver spoons, forks and knives. In the centre of the table was a little arrangement of porcelain jars, each with its own spoon. Elizabeth lifted the lid of one jar; it contained marmalade. It was not quite light outside; blue shadows fell across the table and its spectral setting.

Ross came down some time afterwards, and opened the fridge door. His hair was still wet from his shower. 'Fish paste!' he said.

'Shh!' said Elizabeth. Her eyes were stinging with tiredness. Anna sat on her lap, drinking from her bottle.

'Oh, and look at this. Ham paste. And, hang on –' he reached into the depths of the fridge, bringing out a pale green jar – 'gooseberry jam!'

'There's plenty of jam on the table,' said Elizabeth, nodding at the jars.

'I'll have to try everything.'

When Penny came down she did not talk much, but went about the business of squeezing oranges in a big chrome juicer that stood gleaming by the fridge. She filled all of their glasses with juice – Ross quickly drank down the Ribena he had made himself, and held out his glass.

'I hope you don't mind,' Penny said, 'we've both got appointments today. I thought we could have a picnic in the garden this evening. And perhaps take you out sightseeing tomorrow.'

'No trouble,' said Ross.

'Please don't go out of your way for us,' said Elizabeth.

'We're just happy to be here,' said Ross.

Elizabeth looked sharply at him. He grinned and shrugged slightly.

Upstairs they could hear the shower running, and the sound of a radio in a distant room. Behind them, the conservatory dazzled with morning light. Elizabeth moved all the breakable things out of Anna's reach. There were two morning newspapers on the table; Ross and Penny took one each and read without talking.

By the time Geoffrey came down his fresh orange juice had separated into two parts: a lid of thick orange pulp sat on top of a clearish yellow water. He stirred them together with his silver spoon while Penny boiled him an egg, and drank the orange juice in one draught, putting the glass to the side of the table like a job well done.

Geoffrey began to talk, telling them about Australia, as though they had merely visited it and he was the expert. He had not been there since a business visit in 1975, in the course of which he'd met Penny. He had arrived in the early days of November. He had watched the dismissal on television.

'Australia was lucky,' he said to Ross and Elizabeth. 'The country was being ruined.'

Elizabeth and Ross took a simultaneous deep breath and met each other's eyes. They had both been six year olds during the dismissal but, as the children of Labor voters, had learned to recognise heresy when they heard it.

'He was a whole lot better than the one we've got now,' said Ross.

Geoffrey said, 'Penny was glad to leave.'

Ross opened his mouth again and Elizabeth said, 'May we have more tea?' She frowned at Ross. He closed his mouth.

Anna struggled and slid down from Elizabeth's lap until she was under the table; she had lately become fascinated by the laces on Ross's boots. They could hear her talking to herself, occasionally squeaking with pleasure. The air was full of the smell of toast, and Geoffrey's aftershave. He took *The Times* from Penny's empty place and began to read it. Some birds sang outside. Finally, he stood up, twitching his tie into place.

'We should go, dear,' he said to Penny.

'Yes,' she said.

Ross and Elizabeth stayed sitting at the table while Penny and Geoffrey gathered their coats and Penny her bag. Anna pulled and heaved her way back onto Elizabeth's lap.

'Better take the umbrella,' said Geoffrey, glancing through the window at the clear blue sky.

'Shall we drive your car or mine?' said Penny.

'Are we stopping at the supermarket?' said Geoffrey.

'Can we do any shopping for you?' said Elizabeth. 'Or could we cook dinner?'

'No, no,' said Penny.

'Penny will cook,' said Geoffrey.

'Have you got the key, Ross?' said Penny.

'Yes,' said Ross. 'Remember – you gave it to me last night.'

'Don't worry about the alarm,' said Penny. Instantly a look of regret crossed her face; she had triggered something in Geoffrey.

'Are you sure?' he said, stopping by the umbrella stand.

'It's too complicated, darling.'

'I don't mind,' said Ross.

'But we won't go out for long,' said Elizabeth.

'A burglary can take minutes,' said Geoffrey.

'It's too complicated,' said Penny again, glancing up at the clock. 'I'll miss my appointment.'

'I don't mind having it explained to me,' said Ross, and Elizabeth kicked him under the table.

'It won't take long,' said Geoffrey.

'We absolutely must go,' said Penny, looking again at the clock.

'I'll just show Ross the keypad,' said Geoffrey.

When the door was finally closed behind them there was an airy, fresh smell in the house, displacing the smell of toast. Elizabeth could hear Geoffrey's large, European car starting, and pulling away.

'Jesus,' said Ross, coming back into the kitchen.

'What's the code?' said Elizabeth, feeling her shoulders begin to loosen. Anna nestled against her, bottle still wedged in her mouth.

'I forget,' said Ross. 'I need to do a shit.'

England was so beautiful; Elizabeth had never known this. The air was soft, velvety with summer, but with a delicious lining of cool. She and Ross pushed the pram by the river, which had a path, laid long ago in the green, rich grass, winding through trees heavy with foliage which glittered in the sunlight.

They left the path by the river to walk in the town, where all was pretty and orderly. Cars passed slowly in the little flat streets. People stood back to make way for the stroller as they walked past. In the town they sat in a teashop. Ross ordered scones. The tea – weak and white – came in flowered porcelain of the same ringing delicacy as Penny's. Elizabeth knelt down under the table to clear up Anna's crumbs in a way she never would have in a café at home.

In the afternoon Ross and Anna slept and Elizabeth wandered around the house, her bare feet silent on the inch-thick carpets. You could not hear any noise from the street or the garden. All the windows were closed. The house felt sealed, buffeted. Elizabeth thought of the open windows on their verandah at home, of the continuous passage of air through the house. She was so tired that her eyes ached. She allowed herself to stumble, rather deliciously, feeling the top of one foot graze the soft pile. She put a hand on the white wall to steady herself and took it away to see if she had left a mark.

There were four bedrooms, each with its own bathroom. She paused at the door of Penny and Geoffrey's, with its neat reminders of its occupants; the radio on the bedside table (still talking quietly to itself), the folded nightie, the curtains tied back and letting in the white sunlight. There was a large gilt mirror over the mantelpiece, reflecting Elizabeth where she stood, still and silent, in the doorway. At this distance she could see Anna's face in her own; large dark eyes, their looks made alike by their short hair. Her mouth was small. She opened it and showed her teeth to the mirror.

Superstitious about waking her, Elizabeth did not look in on Anna, and did not stop at the sight of Ross, his back mountainous under the white sheet. In the fourth bedroom she lingered over a bookshelf. Rows of romantic paperbacks, of Daphne du Maurier and Monica Dickens, were occasionally interrupted by a hardback. *The Warren Buffet Way* leaned against *My Cousin Rachel*. There was a black and white photograph of Angela and Penny in a silver frame on top of the shelf. They were young, perhaps fifteen and seventeen, dressed for a dance. Angela had her hair short, Audrey Hepburn's cut, close to her head. Penny's sat out in a pretty circle of manufactured curls.

Even the stairs were carpeted. Elizabeth thought for a second, then sat at the top and allowed herself to slide down, bumping gently on each step, still almost noiseless.

The sunlight had gone from the conservatory, where there were no plants, but a set of outdoor furniture and a table stacked with magazines. Elizabeth sat down at the glass table and pulled a copy of *Woman's Weekly* towards her, her ears tuned for the sound of Anna's voice making its way through the cushioned silences of the house.

In the evening, after Anna had gone to bed, they sat on a picnic rug on the green lawn. Penny had cooked a quiche, with cress from the garden. The twilight went on and on, a deepening of colour, so that the garden seemed to grow richer around them. Penny showed them where the raspberries grew. Elizabeth picked a bowlful, occasionally putting one, gritty and sweet, into her mouth. They ate them with double cream, which curled on the spoon like honey.

By now Ross and Elizabeth were primed for Geoffrey; if he spoke they listened briefly and then changed the subject. Sometimes Elizabeth – astounded at her rudeness (her mother would have been appalled) – gazed over Geoffrey's head when he was talking, or around the garden at the flowers. It was not deliberate; it was survival.

Swamped by Geoffrey the night before, Penny had not mentioned Allan, except to ask about their itinerary in Spain. Now she said to Ross, decorously putting her emptied bowl to one side, 'I hope that your visit with your father goes well.'

It was obvious that this was the most she could bring herself to say, despite the demands of politeness. Elizabeth saw Ross's eyebrows jump up, and expected him to say *Doubt it!* But instead he said, 'I'm not really thinking about it.'

Penny's mouth became thinner.

'He's not expecting to live very long. I said I'd see him before he died.'

The lavender sky was becoming, slowly, a rich violet. Somewhere, an unfamiliar bird made a satisfied little trill. Elizabeth looked down at her hands, and the glass of dessert wine propped between them.

'I haven't seen him since he left,' said Ross.

'He was . . .' said Penny, and paused, stitching her lips even more tightly together.

'He was a bastard,' said Ross. 'You can say it, Penny.'

'I was not going to say that,' said Penny.

'A very selfish man,' said Geoffrey, and Elizabeth stiffened as Ross turned to him, about to speak, but Penny interrupted, saying, 'I can't forgive him.'

Ross looked back at Penny. 'You don't have to. Just because he's got cancer.'

Suddenly Elizabeth choked on a mouthful of wine. Ross hit her, once, on the back.

'Sorry,' said Elizabeth, coughing and swallowing.

Penny bent her head slightly, putting her hand to her brow. Ross looked at Elizabeth, and rolled his eyes.

'Really,' said Ross. 'It's over now.'

'All that time,' said Penny, 'in slavery to that man. And she never said a word. She only told me after he'd gone.'

'What would you have done if she had told you?' said Ross. 'What could you have done, over here?'

'I would have told her to leave him,' said Penny.

'Well, she did in the end,' said Ross. 'And after he left she was very happy. For another fifteen years.'

The bird sang one more pleased little song and Geoffrey said, 'Early start in the morning.'

Ross and Elizabeth tried to help Penny clear up the dishes and plates, but could feel that they were only hindering her. Ross, stalled in his drying and putting away by a piece of kitchen equipment that he did not recognise, stood in the middle of the chequered floor, irresolute. Elizabeth was at the sink.

'That goes in the blender,' said Penny, whisking the curved piece of metal out of Ross's hand, and bending to put it in a cupboard. She turned dials on the dishwasher.

'I think I'll go to bed,' said Ross.

'I won't be long,' said Elizabeth.

The kitchen was white and clean. It was still not completely dark outside. Penny straightened up. 'There,' she said. 'Geoffrey likes to see it tidy.'

Elizabeth pulled the plug and watched the scummy water drain away.

'I'll just set the table,' said Penny.

Elizabeth tried to help, but Penny flapped her away with one hand, so she went back to the kitchen and quietly refilled her glass from the screw-capped bottle in the fridge. Then she stood watching and drinking as Penny hovered over the table, noiselessly placing spoons and plates on the soft white tablecloth. The gloom was deepening; Elizabeth drank the rest of her wine and went upstairs, leaving Penny to her ghostly task.

Ross was asleep and snoring. Elizabeth let her clothes drop onto the floor and climbed into the bed, draping one arm across his broad back. He woke, grunted, and nudged her with his backside. She took her arm away. He began to snore again, and she put her arm back over him. Ross sat up suddenly, throwing her arm off and saying, 'For fuck's *sake*! I was asleep!'

In the morning, after cereal and toast and eggs and orange juice and cups and cups of watery tea, all five of them got into Geoffrey's car to visit a castle. Geoffrey had hired a car seat for Anna and installed it in the centre of the back seat. Ross and Elizabeth sat on either side of her, after a brief discussion about whether Penny should sit in the back 'with the girls'. The low purring of the big car made it possible to talk, but Elizabeth, sleepy after the enormous breakfast, could not be bothered. She was being rude, but they were not her family. She sat looking out of the window and holding Anna's hand as they sped along.

At the castle Elizabeth lagged behind with Anna, no longer caring about manners. The thought of walking through the castle with Geoffrey was intolerable. It was summer, so there were crowds, and Elizabeth had to wait while groups of people bumped past them; a busload of older women, stumping up the battered stone steps; a class of Japanese students, all dressed in dark blue uniforms, the girls sighing delightedly when they saw Anna; a line of intellectually disabled adults, holding each other's hands, some ducking with fright as they passed under the low stone archways.

There was a break then, and Elizabeth put Anna down so that she could crawl up the lumpy steps herself. Sunlight passed through the high, small windows leaving golden shapes on the stone; Anna reached her hand into them, trying to stir the light, or pick it up. Elizabeth could hear people outside on the green lawns. She stood behind Anna, listening, feeling the cool walls under her hands.

Ross was waiting at the stop of the stairs, leaning his back against the wall with his eyes closed. Anna squealed when she saw him and he opened his eyes and smiled.

'You okay?' he said.

'Yeah,' said Elizabeth, 'just taking it slowly.'

Ross picked Anna up and they passed through a little doorway onto a stone terrace. You could lean out between the stones and stare down at the grounds, where people lay in the sunlight or strolled about, silent figures on the green grass. There was a cool breeze.

They caught up with Penny and Geoffrey near

the end of the tour, in the dungeons. Geoffrey, arms folded, was staring into a rectangular hole in the stone floor that showed a tiny, separate dungeon, just big enough for an adult to squat in.

'An oubliette,' said Elizabeth, dredging the word up from somewhere.

'Yes,' said Geoffrey, and started to speak, but Ross interrupted him, peering past him and saying, 'What's it for?'

'They put people in there, put a stone over the hole and just left them,' said Elizabeth, reading the printed sign. 'It sealed them in.'

'Like a Stelvin cap,' said Ross, staring down into the dank space, and Elizabeth tried not to laugh.

'It's from the French,' said Penny, ignoring him. '*Oublier* – to forget.'

'Imagine not being able to move,' said Elizabeth.

It was very dark; you could hear the echo of footsteps as the disabled group climbed back towards the daylight.

They were flying at night again. The air was warm when they stepped out of the crisply airconditioned plane at Madrid – warm and laced with petrol. They allowed themselves to be elbowed into a taxi by an enthusiastic man in a uniform.

'Chueca,' said Ross, and the taxi driver nodded and accelerated away from the pavement with such force that they were thrown back against their seats.

They had been told to expect this, but still it was frightening; the way the taxi driver drove into round-abouts as though they were straight streets, looking neither to the right nor the left. There wasn't a baby seat in the taxi. Elizabeth had known there wouldn't be. She sat behind the driver with Anna grizzling in her lap, the strap of the seatbelt flattened against her hot little back. Elizabeth kept her thigh tensed against Ross's. The traffic at ten pm was a river of yellow light in the darkness. The pavement was alive with people. They could hear music through the taxi's closed windows.

Even Anna fell straight into bed, sleeping beside Elizabeth with one hand caught in her mother's short hair. Some time later Elizabeth woke to feel her eyebrow being stroked. Anna was on all fours in the bed, smiling: deliciously thrilled as she watched Elizabeth wake, breathing her lily breath into her mother's mouth. Elizabeth could see Anna's face in the darkness, the thick lashes and gleam of teeth, and hear her whispering, 'Mum. Mum.' Ross was breathing heavily in the single bed. Sleep came down again like a black curtain.

Madrid in the early morning was airy, empty. The space around them after the confinement of England was dizzying. They pushed the stroller through the centre of town, stopping to look in shop windows at shoes, piles of them. In a back street they came upon a café that was open; it looked as though it had been all night. They sat at the counter and, pointing, managed two cups of earthy coffee and some bread and cheese from the weary-looking owner. Anna sat happily on Elizabeth's lap, stuffing cheese into her mouth with both fists while her parents drank their coffee.

It was bullfighting season. The café was papered with posters, all much the same: the bull plunging, head down, at a stern-featured matador, who swirled his cape over its horns. Ross nodded at the poster behind the bar.

'We should see one,' he said.

Elizabeth finished her coffee and pushed the cup up the counter, away from Anna's reaching hands.

'Don't you think?' said Ross.

'You can if you want.'

'Well, I wouldn't force you to come with me,' said Ross.

'You couldn't,' said Elizabeth.

They argued idly about it as they strolled back to their hotel. Anna dozed in the stroller, her cheeks gluey with cheese.

'You have to respect the bravery of the matadors,' said Ross.

'No I don't.'

'But it's tradition.'

'I don't care.'

Their hotel room was cool and dark, its fitted shutters keeping out the new glare of morning. Anna was asleep in her stroller. They parked it at the foot of the double bed and fell onto the mattress together.

Ross lay behind Elizabeth and brought one hand up to cup her breast. She pushed him away, and he did not argue: they were too tired. They dropped into sleep as the rest of Madrid began to wake. Elizabeth dreamed of movement; of the plane, of traffic, of the lurch of the taxi, her sleep pierced by the sound of horns and sudden voices below.

Ross had decided that they would have a holiday in Spain before seeing Allan. When Elizabeth suggested that it might be better to go south first in case his father's illness moved faster than they expected, Ross said again, 'He can fucking wait.'

Ross showed her the route he had decided upon; they would drive north from Madrid, to the coast and the city of Santiago de Compostela. From Santiago they would start to drive south, heading for Andalusia, taking their time on the long journey through Castile and Extremadura, Spain's western provinces. Elizabeth watched Ross's long finger as it followed the road on the map.

'But we'll be driving in a circle,' said Elizabeth. 'Why don't we just go south from here?' She leaned over the map, pointing at the freeway. 'Through Toledo and Seville?'

'I've already decided,' said Ross.

'Why are you in charge?' said Elizabeth.

'Someone has to be,' said Ross.

Elizabeth thought about being bitterly offended, but said nothing. She did not really mind where they went. It was relaxing, in a way. She took a swig from the bottle of beer Ross had brought up from the bar downstairs. She could not imagine what it must be like to be Ross, to know your own feelings so clearly. She had always been obedient to her mother's precepts first – she tried to be kind, she tried to be generous – saving feeling till later.

Spain was familiar. It was the light, of course: the fierce yellow lion of a sun roaring all day from the sky. The heat, too, slowed people down to an Australian pace, made them seem relaxed and easygoing, brought them to lean over bars, and sit for hours on benches in the shade.

At Leon, they sat outside their hotel at a small metal table. A waiter brought them tall cold glasses of beer. Ross held Anna on his lap. She sat without moving, one hand gripping his index finger. Her face serious, her eyes unblinking as she watched the people moving slowly past.

It was *paseo*, which they had watched from their window the second night in Madrid. All the people dressed up and came out to walk and talk, to sit at the bars and eat tapas or drink cognac. A young couple pushed their pram along the bumpy cobbles, smiling shyly at the glances they attracted. The woman met Elizabeth's eye, with that little exchange of recognition that passes between mothers. The couple's baby lay asleep on a bed of white lace that was piled up around her like cream around a pavlova.

It was a warm evening, with the sky slowly lowering to a darker blue, the lamps coming on around the sloping plaza, people beginning to take their seats at the restaurants. Some men outside a bar had started a game of soccer. A very small boy toddled between them, chasing the ball. The men laughed and encouraged him. One of them stopped and set the ball carefully against a cobblestone, while another held the little boy's hand as he ran up to kick. He missed the first time; a shout of disappointment went up; he kicked again, connected, and all the men cheered.

Ross ordered two tequilas with their next beer. Elizabeth raised her eyebrows.

Ross balanced Anna, a shaker of salt, his glass of tequila. He licked salt from his hand, threw the tequila down, grabbed the lemon and sucked it. 'Excellent,' he said.

The tequila drenched them with warmth. They leaned together and talked. Anna, wide awake, laughed when they made faces and sang to her. When they looked up the plaza was almost empty of strolling people. The restaurants and bars were full. The lamps looked like strings of yellow moons.

After Anna had fallen asleep in her cot Ross turned to Elizabeth in the gloom. She was drunk, had been stumbling happily about the little room, gathering Anna's clothes together and smiling to herself. The sound of people in the street drifted up to them. The air was warm and sweet. Ross put his hands on her hips and pulled her closer, and Elizabeth, feeling her drunk-enness recede, tried to step back. Ross hooked a hand under her bum to tumble her onto the soft hotel bed. If she had been willing, it would have been easy, lovely even, and the bed would have caught her in its yielding embrace. But she resisted, and Ross pulled harder, and she was still too drunk to keep her footing. Instead of falling sideways she fell backwards, catching her foot in the long chenille bedspread and thumping onto the ground, her teeth clashing.

She sat there a moment while her vision settled, then held her hands out to Ross. But he did not respond. He stood watching her, his arms crossed.

'Are you going to help me up?' she said, and Ross said, 'No.'

Elizabeth blinked. 'Why not?' She caught hold of the bedspread and pulled herself up, staggering a little as she reached her feet.

'You're pissed,' said Ross.

'Aren't you?' said Elizabeth, but Ross had already turned away, and was closing the door of the tiny bathroom behind him.

Elizabeth sat down heavily on the side of the bed. She could go after him. She could offer sex. She was so drunk, it would have been easy, really. She cursed herself for resisting. Ross began to run the tap and clean his teeth, and she stood up again, making her way over to the bathroom door, suddenly desperate to fix it, to close up the distance that now yawned between them.

She opened the door and leaned in. Ross turned around, his mouth foaming with toothpaste.

'Sorry,' she said.

He shrugged.

'Do you want to give it another go?'

He spat into the sink and rinsed his mouth and Elizabeth, aware of being punished, waited dumbly.

He straightened up and said to her reflection, cut off at one side of the mirror, 'Forget it. I don't feel like it anymore.'

It took Elizabeth a long time to fall asleep. She was drunk enough to feel the room upending each time she closed her eyes. Eventually she managed to drop off by keeping one eye open, fixed on the solid shadows of the hotel furniture.

The next day Ross bought a sausage at the market, a bright red chorizo made of pork and peppers. The smell filled their hotel room; even the bathroom was rich with the smell of garlic and dried meat. Ross sat with the sausage on a plate in his lap, hacking at it with Elizabeth's penknife. His fingers were stained with red. When he offered some to Anna she would not eat it, lifting her chin and wrinkling her nose.

'What's it like?' said Elizabeth, who had been waiting to break their silence.

'What does it matter to you?' said Ross.

'I'm just asking.'

'Smell it then. It tastes like it smells,' said Ross, and held the sausage out to her. It looked absurdly like a penis, red and fat. They looked at each other. Ross made a stupid sort of thrusting gesture with the sausage, and Elizabeth laughed, feeling her hangover recede as relief trickled in. 'You never miss a chance, do you?' she said.

'I'd never get a fuck if I did,' said Ross.

They smiled carefully at each other, friendship briefly restored.

When the sausage was put away in the mini-bar and Ross had washed his hands, leaving a red stain on the little cake of hotel soap, he climbed onto the soft wide bed with Anna. He lay there with the pillows propped behind his head, Anna beside him, playing with his watch. He was pointing the remote at the enormous television. Elizabeth was standing on a chair, leaning out of their rooftop window, looking along the alley of toppling orange roofs. It was siesta; all the shutters were closed tight against the glare of the sun.

'Hey, look,' said Ross, and she turned round. He gestured with the remote at the tv.

She got down from her chair.

'A bullfight,' said Ross, as she sat down next to him on the yielding bed.

Elizabeth leapt up, clapping her hands over her eyes. 'Ross!'

Ross pressed the button on the remote and the tv's noise was swallowed by silence. 'There wasn't much happening yet,' he said, 'just a lot of galloping up and down.'

Elizabeth was surprised to find herself breathing hard; she reached out for Anna and picked her up, holding her against her chest.

'You alright?' said Ross.

There never seemed to have been a time when she wasn't this sensitive. It was useless, trying to be strict with herself. Once she had seen a dog trotting briskly by a freeway, the traffic streaming so close that the fur on its ears was ruffled. Later she had cried, sure it must eventually have been hit by a car.

'Why didn't you stop and catch it?' said Ross.

'I thought I might frighten it onto the road!' wept Elizabeth.

She had not eaten meat since her teens, unable to bear the weight of so many violent deaths. 'I won't eat anything I can't kill,' she'd said to Ross when they were sitting by the beach one evening.

'So you could kill a fish?' Ross nodded at the crumpled, oily bundle in her lap.

'I think so,' said Elizabeth, but she knew in her heart that she could not.

Sometimes she tried to date her extreme susceptibility from Rita's death, or perhaps from the time of Richard. Ross said she was self-indulgent. She was sure that he was right. It did no-one any good to be keening and wringing her hands while the world and its pain marched by.

'Should I turn it back on?' said Ross. 'It might be good for you.'

'I don't want Anna seeing anything like that,' said

Elizabeth, settling Anna on the other side of her body. 'You can watch if you want. We'll go out.'

'I'm not fussed,' said Ross. 'We can watch something else.' He turned back to the television, flicking it on and changing the channel at the same time. He came to a nature program; a lion grazed on the body of a zebra, then looked up at them, licking its lips.

'This?' said Ross.

'Don't be a dickhead,' said Elizabeth, and Ross flicked through the channels until he found American cartoons, subtitled in Spanish.

From Leon, its warm orange heart radiating streets like rays of light, they drove north to the coast, both longing for the beach after a Sydney winter. However, the farther north they got, the cooler and greyer it became. It soon became apparent that they would not be swimming; Elizabeth dug to the bottom of their suitcases for jumpers and jeans. In bed at night, Elizabeth and Ross slept close together for warmth. Elizabeth wore pyjama bottoms, neither of them acknowledging what this meant.

They spent two nights in Luarca, a small fishing town northwest of Oviedo. They had reached the Celtic part of Spain. The towns were a huddled mass of chalk-white, oddly shaped houses and twisting cobbled streets, and you could buy cider in the bars. Although the sun had broken through the clouds there was a chill in the air, a fishy, dank chill, nothing like the dust and light of Madrid or Leon. Elizabeth shivered deeply when she got out of the car, stiff and cold. 'I need a walk,' she said to Ross.

'Okay. Take Anna, and I'll unload.'

She put Anna's coat on, thought about breastfeeding her but could not face the fumble through her layers of singlet, t-shirt and jumper to find her breast. She took a banana out of her bag and gave her that instead, feeling the milk prickling her nipples. She packed Anna into her stroller and they walked down to the bay.

It was the kind of place where you looked out at the view rather than at what was close by. Heading along the concrete seawall, singing to Anna, Elizabeth gazed at the church on the cliff. It was white and fragile, its cross gleaming where the light caught it. There was a stiff breeze down by the bay; up there it must have been a gale.

The seawall came to an end and Elizabeth sat down for a moment. The sky was growing darker and with it, the sea. There was rain a long way out – she could see it in grey drifts, obscuring the deep blue line of the horizon. Closer in the sun shone fiercely, silvering the choppy water. A seagull flew in front of them and was lit instantly from beneath; its breast was clean, brightly white.

Elizabeth stood and turned back to the town, manoeuvring the stroller on its dodgy wheels over the huge cracks in the concrete. She could feel the rain at her back; the sun was ahead of her, running its eye over each white house on the hill, lighting the blue edges of windows and roof tiles. The water in the tiny harbour, where the fishing boats were moored, had become slickly, ominously still.

A man polishing glasses watched as Elizabeth pushed open the doors to the bar, which was also the hotel's entrance, and used her hip to hold them apart, bumping the stroller up the two steps. Elizabeth smiled and said, '*Hola*,' and he nodded.

Elizabeth opened her mouth to ask him where her room was but the man jerked his head towards an entrance that led onto a long winding corridor.

'*Gracias*,' said Elizabeth. She wondered if she should leave the stroller in the bar, but the man had already turned his back on her. There was a small television in the bar, mounted on the wall high above the tables. The man tilted his head to watch it, his hands still busy with glass and cloth. There was a bullfight on.

The door to the hotel room was open, and Ross was sitting up on a bed with the road map resting on his knees. The room was tiny, twin-bedded, like an unused bedroom in a grandmother's house. The covers were dark green and stiff and smelt of seawater. Ross looked up and smiled as Elizabeth heaved Anna onto her hip, wiping banana off her face.

'Want some help with the stroller?'

'Nup. I'm going to leave it in the corridor.'

'Will that be okay?'

'I think so. It's so quiet – it's like we're the only people staying here,' answered Elizabeth, and sat down next to him, feeling the bed sinking under her as the mattress lost air. Anna leaned forward, trying to grab the edges of Ross's map. He twitched it away.

'What are you up to?' said Elizabeth.

'Just choosing a road.'

'Have you rung your dad?'

'Later on. Tomorrow.'

Outside the window the sky suddenly collapsed into the bay. They both turned to look out. Already you could not see the boats; they were hidden by curtains of water.

The next morning Elizabeth woke struggling to breathe, scrabbling frantically with her fingers at the weight across her face. Ross was still asleep. In her dream a man had been on top of her, forcing the air out of her. She pushed Ross's arm off her. It was still damp with her breath. She sat up in the dim room. Anna turned over in her cot and Elizabeth lay down again immediately, before Anna could see her. She lay stiffly awake for an hour, watching the room fill with light, listening to Ross snoring gently and Anna murmuring to herself.

Ross chose a mountain road for their journey to Santiago instead of the relatively straight and wide coastal road. It took them three hours to drive seventy kilometres along a single lane that wound around the peaks like a track in an anthill. They drove through villages that were dug into the side of the mountain; tiny, steep fields a-topple with cabbages and spinach;

little houses dripping with nasturtiums. The road was so narrow that they could only inch through the villages for fear of knocking down the dogs that wandered skinnily about in the mud, or sideswiping the burros plodding at the roadside, so close that Elizabeth could have run a hand over their hairy flanks. After an hour, Anna began to grizzle; after two hours, with her screams filling the hot interior of the car, Elizabeth demanded that they stop.

Ross pulled over, so that the car was nestled into the mountain, on a part of the road that swelled slightly in order to let others pass. As they stopped, Anna fell silent. It seemed as though the air continued to rush past them; their ears sang.

'I don't think my fingers will unbend,' Ross said, staring down at their grip on the wheel.

'Do it slowly,' said Elizabeth, and opened the car door.

The cold was like a punch in the face. Gasping, she clambered out and made her way round to Anna's door. She unbuckled her and pulled her out, her little legs snagging on the straps. Her back was wet with sweat; feeling the cold, she lifted her head and looked around, her red, tear-streaked face turning from side to side. Elizabeth was shivering. She brought Anna round to the front and climbed back in, pulling the door to and settling her on her lap.

'See if you can find a temperature gauge,' she said to Ross, pulling up her shirt and fumbling with her bra.

While she fed Anna, Ross pressed buttons on the car's display until he found it, switching the clock from time to degrees. It was minus two.

'Fuck,' he said. 'We'd better not stay here too long.'

As he spoke the sky became dark. They turned round to see a huge truck descending the slope towards them. They cowered against the car doors; the truck passed close enough for them to see the angry, distorted face of the driver. The noise was immense; Anna screamed but they could not hear her.

'Change her nappy,' said Ross as the truck howled away. 'We've gotta get moving.'

In Santiago they stayed in a small but luxurious hotel. The cathedral was a few streets away. Its spire looked unreal, like a painting on the sky behind the solid stone buildings that fronted their street.

When they had settled Anna in for her nap they sat at the window. Ross was reading the guide book. Elizabeth looked down at the people in the cobbled street below, trying to feel resolved. Eventually, she took a deep breath and said, 'I think you should ring your father.'

'I was waiting for you to say that,' said Ross, not looking up from his book.

'Sorry.'

'Just leave it to me, okay?'

'But you –'

'I said leave it to me.'

Anna stirred behind them. Elizabeth opened her

mouth to say something more and Ross put a finger to his lips with a tight little shake of the head. Elizabeth stood up and went to lie down on their bed. Anna was asleep with her arms up over head, surrendered. Whole sentences, hybrids of rage and frustration, bloomed in Elizabeth's mind. She stared at the gold-plated fan on the ceiling.

Later they walked up to the cathedral, joining the stream of travellers, some carrying sticks and wearing huge backpacks. At the entrance there was a crowd; Elizabeth had the stroller, and was slow to take her place in the forming line. Ross was behind her.

'Come on!' he hissed, and pushed her shoulder so that she stumbled forward, ramming the stroller wheels into the back of a young man's legs. Elizabeth apologised to the young man and glanced behind her at Ross. He would not meet her eyes – his face was blank. So she bent down and picked Anna up, holding her close so that she could smell her skin.

There was a mass taking place. They watched the swing of the giant censer. Perfumed smoke hung in the air like jellyfish in a quiet sea.

In Salamanca Ross said he would ring his father. Elizabeth took Anna for a walk. It was siesta, but Anna would not fall asleep in her cot. And it was hot again; the light in the middle of the day was like the flash of a huge knife, and the shadows as sharp as if they had been cut out. They crossed the Plaza Mayor, stepping out from the dark corridor of arches into a sea of sunlight. There was no-one around, and the shops were shuttered; Elizabeth could hear the clickety-click of the stroller wheels and her own sandalled footsteps. She pulled the sunshade of the stroller over and then put her hand up to her eyes to cut out the glare. When they reached the other side and the shelter of the arches she was momentarily blinded, and dizzy with heat.

It did not take long to walk to the outskirts of the old town, where the sandstone walls were built high on a hill, and looked over to the river. When Elizabeth lifted the shade to look into the stroller Anna was asleep.

She glanced around. She was alone. There was a breeze here, and swallows cutting past the walls, and a blue sky flooding over her head. She sat down on a wooden bench, unconsciously rocking the stroller with one hand, and crossed her legs.

It was impossible to remember the last time she had been — almost — alone. Her arms still seemed to hold the phantom shape of a baby. Her eyes still felt awash with people; she could hear the disappearing echo of traffic and voices.

Ross was there but not there. Since they'd begun to drive south she had felt him receding; the closer they got to his father the more silent he became, the more difficult to speak to. He looked past her when they sat in bars, trying to drink themselves into a cheerier place. Following his gaze, she nearly always found that he was watching television; and on the television there would be sport. Soccer, or a bullfight. She could feel herself and Anna dropping out of sight for him, like people standing beside an accelerating car.

Eventually the noise and colour ebbed away and there was nothing, except the slight, hollow swoop of the swallows and the river rustling in the distance. Anna slept without moving. Elizabeth turned her face into the breeze. She could feel the wooden bench pressing into her legs. She closed her eyes.

'It's the same one,' Ross announced when she walked in, Anna asleep in her arms. He was sitting in front of the tv, with the sound down. The position of his body – arms flat along the sides of the chair, legs apart – showed that he had been waiting for her.

Elizabeth shook her head and frowned down at the sleeping child. She lowered Anna onto the mattress of the king-sized bed, and pulled a sheet over her. Her back hurt. 'Let's go out on the verandah,' she whispered to Ross. He nodded and stood up to follow her out.

Their hotel was three floors up, taking up a small part of the rich, ornate sandstone building whose four sides bounded the Plaza Mayor. The verandah did not feel safe, but this was Spain. You were kept from falling by iron lace as high as Elizabeth's waist; rickety iron lace that tilted forward when you leant on it. Siesta was over and groups of people were appearing in the plaza below, drifting together and apart like coloured oil on the surface of water.

They sat down. 'What's the same one?' said Elizabeth, and leaned her sore back into her chair.

Ross was important with anger. 'The same woman he was having an affair with when he was married to Mum. He's still with her.'

'I thought he had a nurse.'

'It's her. She's looking after him. I spoke to her.'

Elizabeth put her hand out to touch Ross's, but he moved it into his lap. She said, 'She's probably not having such a great time with him now.'

Ross looked away from her; he stared through the iron lace at the people below. 'Who gives a fuck about that? I hope he hit her as much as he hit Mum.'

For a moment Elizabeth did not speak. Then she said carefully, 'You don't really think that.'

'Don't fucking tell me what I think. I know how I feel about it. I'm not the one in denial.'

Elizabeth felt herself go cold. 'In denial about what?' she said.

'Whatever,' said Ross, with a savage gesture. 'Everything.'

He was simply taking a swipe at her, not talking about anything in particular. Elizabeth steadied herself, and said, 'Did you ever meet her?'

'Once. She came to help him with his stuff when he left. Mum went out, but I stayed.' He took hold of the iron lace.

'What's her name?' said Elizabeth.

'Loli,' said Ross, and shook the iron lace back and forth so that it squeaked and banged. 'Short for Dolores.'

Anna woke with a cry.

'Fuck!' said Ross, and stood up, but Elizabeth put a hand out, glad to have a reason to walk away. 'I'll do it,' she said.

The tv was still on; as Elizabeth stepped back into the hotel room she glanced at the screen. A black bull, head lowered, wheeled and charged across a dusty expanse. Elizabeth quickly turned her back. She wondered if Anna had been watching. She was smiling – grinning, now she had seen Elizabeth – and lifting her legs together to whump! whump! down on the mattress.

'Hello, my gorgeous,' said Elizabeth, feeling behind her for the tv. Her fingers found the power switch. She pressed it, and reached down to pick Anna up.

Ross had not spoken to his father. 'He wasn't in bed, though,' he said, standing framed in the doorway. It was hard to see his face; the sun was fierce behind him. 'He'd gone into town. I thought he was supposed to have cancer.'

Elizabeth, with Anna's head resting in her palm, held her by the back of the neck and aimed her, mouth open, at her breast. She took hold – the little suck then squelch! of attachment, hardly changed since her early days of babyhood – and instantly her body relaxed into Elizabeth's arms. Elizabeth turned her face up to Ross's. 'Maybe he was seeing a doctor,' she said.

The silhouette of Ross put its hands on its hips. It stood there a moment, saying nothing. And then filled up, became solid, as Ross stepped into the room and sat heavily down on the bed next to Elizabeth, almost, but not quite, jouncing Anna's mouth from her mother's breast.

The hotel room was a suite; it had an adjoining room, tiny, with a couch and a shiny little coffee table. The hotel had put a cot in there, and after Anna had fallen asleep in it they got into the huge bed. It dipped in the middle, so that Elizabeth could not stop herself rolling towards Ross.

They had closed the doors and the shutters. The room was so dark it was like being in a warm black sea, like swimming on a tropical night. When Ross slid his hand onto Elizabeth's thigh she knew she should not resist. She could not face the fight that would follow.

Afterwards they lay on their backs, Ross with one hand heavy on Elizabeth's stomach. Milk was leaking from her breasts, soaking the sheets like tears. Ross was asleep in minutes. Elizabeth could see the red power light from the tv, unwinking in the blackness.

The next morning there was more kindness, as though the light loosened things. Elizabeth and Ross kissed when they woke, although they didn't talk, as they usually did, before bringing Anna into their bed. But her warm body between them, the way she joined them by holding them both, made it feel as though they were still together. When Elizabeth turned her head she could see the curve of Anna's cheek and the bat, bat of her eyelashes as she lay there. She was, sometimes, impossibly serene. She could lie unmoving for a long time. Was she thinking? And what?

It was hot, even hotter than the day before. They stayed indoors for the first half of the day, watching children's television and playing games to amuse Anna. Ross hid in the bathroom – suddenly he leapt out, hands hooked like claws, grinning madly. Anna squealed and tried to crawl away, looking over her shoulder and screaming with laughter as he caught her round the tummy and tickled her.

While she slept Ross read the guide book and found the town's municipal pool, which was on its outskirts. 'We could walk it,' said Ross. Neither of them wanted to take the car out of the hotel car park and try to negotiate the spaghetti of streets that made up the old town.

They set off in the middle of the afternoon, walking slowly through the dry heat. The streets were oddly empty – perhaps siesta was longer on a Saturday. They sang to Anna as they passed from the gently glowing sandstone centre out into the blue-grey rings of newer buildings, where the streets were narrow and cavernous, cutting out some of the blinding sun.

It was busier here. People began to appear in the dark doorways, parking cars and climbing out, coming from cafés and bars. There was intent in the air. Everyone was walking in the same direction. Everyone was well dressed, happy, excited. Ross and Elizabeth dodged the long slabs of sunlight to walk in the shade, along the edges of buildings. There were old couples (even, here and there, an elderly lady wearing her hair in a mantilla, her arm linked in her husband's as they walked regally along), families, teenagers in groups.

Elizabeth and Ross rounded a corner and it became immediately apparent where the increasing crowd was heading. Distinct from the dark buildings around it, the Plaza de Toros was made of light stone that called to the honey colours of the town's old centre. Its curved wall stood high against a nursery blue sky. Swallows dipped and dived around the flags that flapped on its tallest reaches.

The crowd was moving faster here – a teenage boy caught his girlfriend's hand and ran her across the road before the lights had changed. People began to produce tickets from pockets and bags. The base of the huge structure had doors cut into it, where uniformed men stood, collecting tickets. Groups of people hailed each other. Children screamed with delight, clutched at each other, swung on their parents' hands. You could hear the rumble of thousands of voices behind the yellow walls.

Ross stopped, and Elizabeth bumped into him. 'Let's not go to the pool. Let's go to the bullfight,' he said. He stared across the street at the people streaming into the Plaza de Toros.

Elizabeth looked at the people too. 'I'd really rather not,' she said, still aware of being careful. She peered down the road for cars.

'But it's right here! We could just walk in.'

Elizabeth, thinking fast, said, 'It'll terrify Anna.'

'You're a fucking killjoy,' said Ross.

Elizabeth thought about love, and familiarity. How a beloved face could become a hated one. This particular tight look that Ross had, his mouth white around the lips, and small with contempt. She said, 'I really think it would be horrible.'

'How would you know? You've never seen one.'

'I can imagine it.'

They stared at each other.

Elizabeth looked at her feet. Then she said, 'You could go, and we could meet you on the way back.'

'I'm not going on my own,' said Ross.

Elizabeth paused. The temptation was enormous; if she gave in Ross would be soothed, and pleased with her. She was exhausted. 'I can't do it,' she said at last.

Ross folded his arms.

'Let's just go to the pool,' said Elizabeth. 'It's so hot.'

Ross still said nothing.

'Maybe you could go with your dad.'

Ross shrugged, then said, 'Whatever.' He elbowed her aside and took the stroller. There was a break in the traffic, and he crossed without warning, forging ahead so that Elizabeth had to trot to keep up with him.

The pool was set in worn, grassy grounds, in its own enclosure, with a steel fence and a little shower in a cage that you had to run through to get inside.

'To get the dirt off you,' said Ross, reading the sign fixed to the fence.

The shower water came down hard and sharp as spears, and freezing. Elizabeth kept her body bent over Anna's as they ran through. She screamed; she couldn't help herself. Ross ran after her, catching at her waist and pushing her in front of him in his haste to get past the piercing water. They sat gasping on the edge of the pool, their legs dangling, trying to get used to the cold. A teenage boy and girl, oblivious, stood embracing in the shallow end, their hands swarming over each other. The sun beat down on their heads.

It was nearly six hundred kilometres from Salamanca to the mountains where Allan lived – half as far as they had driven in the past week – but Ross decided that they would make the journey in a day.

'It's too long for Anna to be in the car,' said Elizabeth as they sat on the verandah that night. Ross was still distant with her; when she'd tried to kiss him he'd held his lips together, so that her mouth bumped dryly against his. She was drinking a bottle of beer. She had told herself not to let him upset her.

'We'll stop every couple of hours and find somewhere for her to have a crawl,' said Ross.

Elizabeth paused, and took a swig of beer. She was

still having to choose her words cautiously. 'I don't understand why we're in a rush all of a sudden,' she said.

The plaza's golden lamps had come on. A group of musicians passed from bar to bar, strumming guitars and singing into the warm night air.

Ross stared down at them. 'I've just had enough.'

'Of me?' said Elizabeth in a small voice.

He glanced at her irritably. 'No. For fuck's sake. I just need to get it over and done with. I can't concentrate till it's done.'

She met his eye.

'I *know*,' he said. 'I can change my mind, can't I?'

There was the sound of chairs being scraped back as people stood up to dance with the musicians. Someone began clapping, flamenco style.

Elizabeth drank more beer. 'Okay. I just hope Anna doesn't scream the whole way.'

'She'll be fine.'

Miraculously, he was right. Anna slept most of the time as they sped along freeways, through landscape that changed from mountains to desert to flat plains of yellow grass. When they stopped they sat in cafés whose stone floors and small windows kept them cool. Anna crawled about picking up the little twists of sugar paper discarded by coffee drinkers. The towns they drove through during siesta were deserted, houses and shops shut up as though a posse had just ridden through and slaughtered all the inhabitants. Every so often, like a thundercloud in the distance, then looming right on top of them, was the enormous silhouette of a black fighting bull, propped up from behind with wooden poles.

At a petrol station and restaurant that took up an acre of dirt, Ross emerged from paying for petrol with two tall bottles of beer. He was cheerful and smiling, as he had been since they'd left Salamanca. Elizabeth despised herself for feeling so grateful.

'I love this country!' said Ross, handing the freezing bottles to Elizabeth and pulling his door shut. 'Who else would think to sell alcohol to people driving?'

They drank the beer and ate a packet of chips as they drove up the mountain road from Seville, towards Allan's farm. They sang to Anna, who was awake now, and jolly. She pointed at cows and horses as they slipped past the car windows.

'Are you nervous?' said Elizabeth to Ross.

Ross accelerated past a truck loaded with dark, hairy pigs. 'Why should I be nervous?' he said, raising his arm to the truck driver. 'I didn't do anything wrong.'

They drove past the entrance twice before seeing it, then slowly up a winding dirt drive, under willow trees that hung in front of the windscreen as though they were trying to peer in at the occupants. Elizabeth's mouth was dry and tasted of stale beer. She looked sideways at Ross, who had not spoken for the last ten kilometres. He was leaning forward – there was a space between his back and the car seat.

They drove through a stone arch past the house and parked the car next to an old brown Renault. They sat there for a second, quietly. Elizabeth turned round to look at Anna, who was watching them with a grown-up, quizzical smile on her face.

They walked, stiff with fatigue, back through the arch to the house, Elizabeth carrying Anna. Ross had his hand on the back of Elizabeth's neck, pressing, so that her head was forced slightly forward. It had begun as a gesture of affection, or at least solidarity; as they reached the big red doors it was hurting and Elizabeth had to straighten her neck and shake him off. Ross stepped in front of her and knocked. They waited, in a slowly expanding silence.

The woman who answered the door had caramel-coloured hair. She was fiftyish, short, with solid hips and a big bony nose. 'Ross?' she said, her accent thickly Spanish.

'Is he here?' came a loud male voice from behind her, and Ross moved suddenly backwards, so that he stepped on Elizabeth's foot, her face colliding with his sweaty back.

'Sorry,' he said, putting a hand behind him to touch her, and out of the gloom behind Loli appeared his father.

'G'day,' he said, 'did you have a good trip?'

Elizabeth left Ross sitting next to his father on the big red couch in front of the widescreen television, his third beer gripped tightly in his fist. Anna had at last had enough; offered dinner, she'd smacked Elizabeth's hand away so that baked beans flew across the kitchen. Loli raised her eyebrows and went on scrubbing potatoes at the sink. Elizabeth opened a little tub of yoghurt and Anna shrieked, twisting so that she slipped down between Elizabeth's legs and onto the tiled floor. Before Elizabeth could put the yoghurt down, Anna had pulled herself to standing by hanging on to her mother's knees, and hit her head on the underside of the table. The screams succeeded each other as Elizabeth carried her out of the kitchen, leaving the baked beans and the yoghurt on the table and the floor. As she passed she put her head into the living room; Ross was getting to his feet.

'Shall I come?' he said, putting his beer down.

'No, don't. Stay there. I'll put her straight to bed.'

Ross nodded, and sat back down. Allan did not turn around. The news was on.

Their room was at the top of the house. It was tiled, with arched windows that looked across a thickly wooded mountain. The evening was still light; that faintly purple twilight that would last for hours now they had reached the south. Elizabeth pulled the curtains and laid Anna on the bed to undress her. By now her screams were hurting Elizabeth's ears, and making her heart rattle wildly in its cage. Anna kicked out as Elizabeth pulled her pants off, thumping both feet into her mother's breasts. Elizabeth's own tiredness rose in her body suddenly, and she had to suppress the urge to shout back at her. She kept one hand firmly on Anna's heaving chest, stripping, changing, until, at last, she was ready to feed.

Anna was asleep in seconds, her fingers twisted firmly into the back of Elizabeth's hair, her breath coming in little sobbing gasps as she sucked. Elizabeth had not had time to find a comfortable position. Her back sagged and ached. She tried to sit up straight.

She could hear Loli in the stone courtyard, setting the long wooden table. The television downstairs, turned up so that Allan could hear it. And somewhere a burro, its bray coursing absurdly across the valley.

Allan was shorter than Ross, with darker skin and a face pitted by alcohol. Their features were the same; dark brown eyes, curving, shapely lips, noses a little too big, but Ross looked contained, upright, where Allan was squatter, like a melted figure of his son. His stomach was large, but unnaturally so. He wore the top button of his shorts undone. His hair was thin and the skin under his eyes was a greenish yellow.

Ross and Allan both drank steadily at dinner, while Loli refilled their glasses and returned with more and more dishes of food. There was dried salt cod that had been soaked in water but was still chewy; Elizabeth could not like it, though she swallowed it gamely, feeling the hard lumps of fish battle their way down her throat. There were fried potatoes. There was a soup made from almonds and garlic. There was pasta, with fat olives and tomatoes that Loli had dried in the sun. Elizabeth had seen the split log that she laid them on, at the kitchen's back door.

Loli did not speak much, and nor did Elizabeth. She was so tired that the wine they drank was making her feel as though her bones were liquefying. She kept sitting up straighter, imagining herself sliding under the table. Ross and Allan talked, but not as though they had things to catch up on. They discussed Elizabeth and Ross's trip through Spain. Allan told them they had been ripped off on their car hire. He said that Santiago was better in the winter.

Later that night Elizabeth and Ross lay side by side in bed.

'I'm so drunk,' whispered Ross, 'I can't close my eyes.'

'Take deep breaths,' said Elizabeth.

Ross grabbed her hand and squeezed it, taking a huge, racking breath. He smelled of beer. His hand was slightly clammy.

'Are you feeling okay?' she said a minute later, but he did not hear her. Soon his snores were mingled with the pale, quiet breathing of Anna, asleep in her cot where she had been set down, her little mouth open like a shell.

In the early morning Loli drove Allan to the hospital in Seville, but they were back for lunch. Elizabeth had spent the morning playing on the floor with Anna while Ross lay on the bed, occasionally groaning. She built a cubbyhouse out of the chairs in their bedroom and draped the sheets across them. Anna, crawling faster than ever, scuttled under the chairs and crouched there. They could hear her holding her breath, trying not to laugh. When Elizabeth snatched up the sheet and thrust her head under to grin at her, Anna screamed with delight.

Loli had made gazpacho in the morning. Again they ate at the table in the stone courtyard, with Loli silently waiting on them. Ross poured himself a large glass of wine, and held out an arm so that Elizabeth could hand Anna to him. He settled her carefully on his lap. 'Shouldn't you be lying down?' he said to Allan.

'I'm alright,' said Allan. But he did not eat much. When Loli cleared the table his dish was still full, his bread unbroken in front of him. He drank continuously.

'So,' he said, as Loli backed into the house with her piled tray, 'how's your mother?'

Elizabeth looked at Ross.

His eyes widened, momentarily. 'She's dead,' he said.

Allan looked startled, but then he smiled, a slightly embarrassed smile. 'Oh,' he said, 'that's a surprise.'

'I wondered if you'd know,' said Ross. He bent his head for a moment, putting his lips into Anna's hair so that they could not see his eyes.

'How would I know? None of her friends would talk to me. You wouldn't talk to me. This is quite a shock.' Allan poured some more wine. 'What did she die of?'

Ross lifted his face and met his father's gaze. 'Cancer. Ovarian cancer.'

'Not the breasts, then. That can be hard for a woman.'

'Dad,' said Ross.

'What? What did I say?' said Allan.

'Forget it,' said Ross.

'Your mother had beautiful breasts,' said Allan, and Ross said, 'Give it a rest, will you?'

Allan raised his eyebrows, as though politely censuring poor behaviour, and said nothing more. The three of them sat on in silence. Ross gave Anna his dessert spoon to play with.

Loli came back with a plate of cheese. Elizabeth took a breath and said to Allan, 'What kind of cancer do you have?'

Allan looked her squarely in the eye. 'Prostate.'

Loli's English was perfect, though heavily accented. She had lived in Australia for ten years, working in marketing. In fact, she had been Allan's colleague in their office in Chatswood, working on the same floor with the other consultants. Elizabeth did not learn any of this from Loli, who rarely spoke. Allan talked about her as though she was not there, or as though she couldn't speak English at all. He was peculiarly thick-skinned. He ignored Ross's long, rude silences, and his scornful rejection of his father's opinions on politics and sport. Elizabeth had expected someone humble, supplicatory, desperate to see himself exonerated before he died. But Allan treated Ross as though nothing but separation had occurred. He seemed to enjoy their disagreements; it was as though he had missed fighting with him, but all the rancour that must have existed between the teenager and the forty year old had gone, and Allan laughed when Ross abused him.

Ross seemed as content as Allan to leave the past alone; when Elizabeth suggested, again, that he should talk to him about it, Ross was dismissive. 'It wouldn't work,' he said. 'And anyway, he's not worth it.'

Elizabeth did not say anything more after this. She and Ross had been at peace since they'd arrived at Loli's house, probably because of the interposing of Allan between them. They had not talked about themselves, or about sex. But nor had they fought since reaching the farm.

Sometimes Allan looked narrowly at Elizabeth when he thought she wouldn't notice, as though he knew what she thought of him, or as though he was sizing her up to see if she would do as a daughter-in-law. But still, there was no urgency in the way he behaved towards any of them. And he never spoke about being sick.

Loli and Ross did not even look at each other. Ross had put aside his father's transgressions against his mother, but he had not forgotten Loli's part in them, or that was the way it seemed. Ross thanked her for every carefully prepared lunch and dinner that she brought them, and in response, Loli nodded. They never touched. Elizabeth watched them holding their bodies carefully apart if one had to pass the other.

155

It was surprising, how easily time passed, while this silence existed. Loli did not bother to contribute to their conversation, which was fairly lively when Ross and Allan were in charge. She sat still and expressionless as they talked, moving only to hand round more food or more wine.

On the third night things changed again. Ross came to bed late, when Elizabeth was deeply asleep. She was woken by the feel of his hands trailing up her body to her breasts. She was too sleepy to speak; she pushed his hand away and shifted further over in the bed. Ross came after her, putting his face in the back of her neck and slipping his fingers between her legs. She slapped at him as she would a fly.

'Come on,' he whispered.

'Too tired,' mumbled Elizabeth. She moved so that one arm dangled off the edge of the bed.

Ross slid down the bed, putting his face on her stomach, tickling her pubic hair.

'Don't!' said Elizabeth, wriggling out from under him. 'I'm asleep!'

'You are not!' said Ross.

'I don't feel like it! Okay?'

Ross took his hands away and moved back over to the other side of the bed. 'You could make an effort.'

'I'm tired,' said Elizabeth, making a show of pulling the sheet over her again.

'Yeah, yeah,' said Ross. 'You always say that.'

'You fucking woke me up!'

They lay there, each determined not to move,

caught in their poses of rejection. Elizabeth could feel the blood beginning to make her ear hot against the pillow. It felt impossible, at times like this, to try fixing things. To move her hand and touch Ross. She stayed still, her legs aching, and was nearly asleep when Ross said, 'I can't put up with this for much longer.'

She pretended not to have heard him, though she knew this must be true. But if he hadn't asked, if he hadn't made this move, the brief peace between them could have gone on.

When she woke the room was full of new blue light, and she did not know what she had dreamed, except that it had left shame and discomfort in the air. Ross lay apparently fast asleep, his back to her. Anna squawked from her cot and Elizabeth sat up, into the beginning day.

Allan had a stick, which he sometimes carried as he would a furled umbrella, under his arm and pointing at the person behind him. He leaned on the stick if they were going down stairs, or standing somewhere for any length of time.

Allan's stick was collapsible. It was quite difficult to work; the four separate pieces could be pulled apart and folded into each other, but only with great effort. Elizabeth and Allan couldn't do it; Ross and Loli could.

However, the stick reassembled itself in a split second – too easily – when you pressed the button underneath its hook. In fact you didn't have to press it;

merely brushing it made the stick leap to attention, snapping itself into shape. Elizabeth would not let Anna touch it. She sat on the couch with Anna held firmly on her lap while Ross collapsed the stick and then pressed the button. The stick shot into place so fast it could have broken a leg.

'Look at this,' said Ross, doing it again. 'Quick on the draw, eh?'

They had to be careful. If Allan left the stick folded and lying around, and someone knocked against it as they walked past, it assembled itself, shooting across the floor like a snake from a hole.

The house was full of silences. Elizabeth would stand in the empty corridors, listening, hearing her heart in her ears, wondering if she was alone. Sometimes Allan and Loli lay in the shade under the chestnut trees. Sometimes their car was gone and Ross and Elizabeth found their own food in the kitchen, moving quietly about on its stone floor as though they were trespassing.

Elizabeth watched Allan and tried to imagine him being violent. It was very difficult. He never lost his temper, a feat he seemed able to manage by not particularly liking or approving of anything. He was already disappointed – he could not be more so.

But Ross had said that when he was a boy there had been days when the only thing to do was leave the house; when a book left open on a sofa instead of closed and on the shelf would be the start of a rage that could end in all the books being torn from the shelves and flung onto the floor. And later, Angela, crying quietly, kneeling and restoring them to their place, while Allan, apparently sated, took the car and went out for a drink.

Allan appeared to have nothing of the hothead left in him. Like an office building at night, various parts of him were shutting down, switching off. Perhaps the rage had been the first to go.

In keeping with the rest of his behaviour, Allan seemed to have no passion for Anna. He pointed out that she looked like Angela and was silently tolerant when she dribbled food on the couches and screamed in the middle of the night. If she crawled towards him he kept still until she crawled away. He never asked to have her sat on his lap, the way most people did – and Elizabeth dreaded them doing, for Anna always cried and reached out for her parents. Loli, too, paid very little attention to Anna.

Elizabeth took over most of Anna's care, glad she had something to do, somewhere to be. They played together in the upstairs bedroom, where the clear air trembled over the trees and the cicadas shouted from their branches. Anna was at her best in these quiet times; the presence of all the adults seemed to over-excite her, as though she was the only one expressing the tension that remained unvoiced by any of them. At mealtimes especially she would bounce herself up and down on Ross's lap, giving out her high-pitched scream, or scramble breathlessly away from him and towards some lurking danger; a pot full of plants, ready to be toppled, or the edge of the pond.

Elizabeth and Ross slept in the same bed but did not touch, or if they did, moved apart. Elizabeth's sleep was light, her whole body aware of this. She woke every morning exhausted from keeping herself still and away from Ross.

One morning, after she'd been breastfeeding, she sat in the chair by the window with Anna on her lap and looked out at the valley. She had taken her t-shirt off to feed; it was so hot, and easier to get at her breasts without it. Anna sat twirling the fingers of one hand in Elizabeth's hair, and with the other gently patting Elizabeth's bare bosom. She was nearly asleep.

Elizabeth heard the sound of boots on the stairs. She knew it must be Ross, so did not move to rearrange herself. He opened the door. She looked up at him.

'What are you doing?' he said.

'Just getting Anna ready for bed.'

'I thought you might want to come for a walk.'

'Where are the others?'

'Gone out.'

'But we can't leave Anna alone in the house.'

'We won't go far. Just down to the stream.'

Elizabeth shook her head.

'We're supposed to be on *holiday*. We're supposed to have some time together. Have you forgotten about that?'

'We can sit downstairs and have coffee. And a chat,' said Elizabeth.

Ross said, 'We could have sex.'

'Where?'

'*Where?*' said Ross in a high-pitched voice, savagely imitating her. 'I don't know. Fuck it. Forget about it.'

Anna had fallen asleep, one hand now tucked under Elizabeth's breast. Ross looked pointedly at it. 'At least someone gets to touch them,' he said, and turned away, closing the door behind him, before Elizabeth could say anything more.

When Anna was in her cot Elizabeth ran silently downstairs, her heart beating too fast. She looked in the living room, the kitchen, the big white bathroom, but Ross was not there. She went round to the back of the house and saw him standing by the pond.

The pond had seven white geese on it, each the size of a cattledog. The geese had pale blue eyes and orange beaks, and did everything together, sailing across the water as though pulled by the same string, marching shoulder to shoulder over the mud. If you stepped out of the house while they were afloat on the pond they would all swerve towards you, beaks pointing your way, like weathervanes.

Ross lifted an arm and the geese backed away.

Elizabeth stepped out of the house and crossed the yard to where he stood. 'I think we need to have a talk.' Her whole body could feel the cold pump of blood.

Ross crossed his arms. 'Do you?'

Elizabeth took a breath so deep it hurt her throat. 'I'm sorry,' she said. 'I'm sorry about the sex thing.'

It was hot and still, although a little birch tree rattled its leaves at them as an imperceptible breeze passed through it.

'I'm finding it difficult,' Elizabeth went on. She stepped her feet slightly apart, trying to plant herself.

'You don't say,' said Ross.

The geese paddled, floating, watching them. Elizabeth tried to sound more resolute, saying, 'But I think I know why. I mean, I can explain it.'

Ross didn't look at her. 'Don't bother,' he said.

Elizabeth was pulled up short. She stared at his set profile, his nose jutting sharply. 'What do you mean?' she said.

'I don't care why you can't have sex. I'm sick of caring about it. I'm not going to fucking leave you,' he said, turning to see the stricken look on Elizabeth's face, 'I just don't want to talk about your problems right now. I've been generous, I've been nice, and now I'm sick of it.'

'But –' said Elizabeth.

'We'll talk about it when we get home.'

'But I want to tell you something. It's important.' She was blinking back tears.

Ross kicked some dirt into the water. 'To be honest, I really don't give a shit. Right now, let's just deal with Dad. He could be dead in a week.'

Still blinking, Elizabeth said, 'Do you think so?'

Ross laughed nastily. 'I hope so. We've got to get back for the start of semester.'

Elizabeth had never imagined this; that her attempt to explain, to finally tell about what she was

162

really like, would be repulsed. When Ross left her, saying he was going for a walk whether she wanted to or not, she sat down quite suddenly in the dirt, making all the geese flurry towards the other side of the pond. She felt so humiliated that she could hardly move or even breathe; she stared down at her fingers. Her tears, unshed, sat coldly in her eyes.

A great deal of time seemed to pass. The geese floated closer to her, eyeing her, paddling. She stood up stiffly, and the geese backed away, though there was no need for panic this time. Her hips and legs hurting, and her head held rigidly on her shoulders, Elizabeth went into the house. Slowly she climbed the stairs. Anna would be awake soon.

That afternoon, needing very much to keep out of Ross's way, Elizabeth carried Anna down the goat track through the sloping paddocks to show her the pigs. The light was silver and clear, mountain light. Goats and sheep lifted their heads from the grass to watch her as she picked her way past them. Sometimes a sheep could not bear it, and broke into a stumbling run as she approached, its hooves making little thuds on the soft earth. The goats stood their ground, smiling insolently.

The house was Loli's, Allan had told them. When her parents died she and her brother Paulo had inherited the whole farm. Loli invested her superannuation, Paulo ran the farm, and together they made a comfortable living by it. Paulo, who was much younger than his sister, lived in the house in the valley.

He kept huge black Iberian pigs, fed on the chestnuts that grew over the whole property.

The pigs had the run of half the valley, but were kept from Paulo's house by a long wire fence. They stood or lay in the shade, twitching flies from their vast hairy flanks. Paulo came out of his house, dressed for town, and saw Elizabeth standing there, Anna in her arms.

They smiled at each other, awkwardly; Paulo was much friendlier than Loli, but spoke even less English than Elizabeth did Spanish.

'They look hot,' said Elizabeth, nodding at the pigs. '*Calor.*'

'*Sí,*' said Paulo. His truck was parked by the house; he looked towards it, and then back at Elizabeth.

Elizabeth started to say, 'I feel sorry for them,' but stopped herself, thinking it sounded stupid.

Paulo moved forward, pointing at something. 'You –' he said, and she followed his gaze. He was pointing at the hose, hanging in loops from the wire fence. 'You – water,' said Paulo.

Elizabeth laughed. 'Water the pigs?' she said.

Paulo nodded.

'Is that okay? You won't mind?'

He understood her perfectly, and said something in Spanish that she could not translate. She smiled and settled Anna on one hip, taking the hose that Paulo offered her. He turned it on, and she swung the rope of water over the pigs. 'Lovely,' she said, 'thank you. *Gracias.*'

'*De nada*,' said Paulo, and turned away to his truck. He drove off, barrelling through the dust, and Elizabeth moved closer to the fence. Some of the pigs were hauling themselves to their feet, coming towards her. A young one brought its snout right against the wire, and Elizabeth clutched at Anna, who was beginning to slip off her hip. Anna reached out with her little fingers, pink and sweet like baby prawns, so crunchable. Elizabeth set her down in the dirt, just far enough away so that a snaggle-toothed mouth could not force through the wire to her. The young pig closed its eyes as Elizabeth directed the water over its back. Soon there was a wide wallow of mud, and the pigs seemed to be grinning at them. Anna said, 'Oink', and the pigs responded with deep, delighted grunts, preening their bristly bodies under the drop and slap of water.

In the late afternoon, Elizabeth sat alone at the table in the courtyard. Ross was watching tv with Anna. In the kitchen Elizabeth had poured herself a gin and tonic, with the Spanish gin that Loli and Allan kept in the freezer. She'd seen it for sale in the supermarket; it cost about ten dollars for a litre. It tasted faintly of petrol. The effect was cold and almost painful to the throat, but it made you drunk very quickly.

She turned around at the crunch of feet on the stones of the terrace. Allan was approaching, carrying his own gin and tonic, leaning on his stick.

'Thought I'd join you,' he said.

165

Elizabeth stood up and helped him into a chair. Some of his drink slopped onto his knees; having settled himself, he wiped the drops carelessly with the heel of one hand.

This was the first time Elizabeth had been alone with Allan. She felt her stomach turning nervously, and took a sip of her drink, but Allan did not seem worried. He said, 'Ross tells me you've been to England.'

Elizabeth nodded, making the ice cubes in her drink click.

'To see Penny,' said Allan.

'Yes. Have you met Penny?' said Elizabeth politely.

'Oh yes,' Allan chuckled. 'She didn't like me.'

It was the first time anyone had referred, obliquely or otherwise, to the past. Elizabeth, made a little reckless by the gin, said, 'How could you tell?'

Allan took a swig of his own drink. 'Signs,' he said. 'She wouldn't touch me. They were always hugging and kissing everybody, Angela and Penny. Except me! Penny wouldn't come near me.'

Elizabeth did not know what to say. Penny had not tried to touch either her or Ross. Or Anna.

'Then she met that dickhead and moved to England. That would have been when Ross was five. Or six.'

'Did Angela miss her?' asked Elizabeth.

'I don't know. She didn't say.'

'They only saw each other once more,' said Elizabeth. 'When Angela was dying.'

'Really? Well, Penny was a pain in the arse. I don't blame Angela for that.'

'They wrote to each other. I think they just didn't get round to it before that.' Elizabeth drank from her glass, and the ice hit her teeth.

'See that mountain over there?' said Allan, using his stick to point. The mountains were a deep green in the distance. The light was clear, glittering.

'We had fires one year, for months. Nothing dramatic. The farmers kept them contained. The side of that mountain had been smouldering all afternoon, but nobody was paying any attention. I was just standing here, looking at it, when the whole lot went whoomp! Just like that! Like someone had dumped a truckload of kerosene on it.'

An eagle came drifting past, its wings embracing air.

Allan put his stick down and finished his gin, swallowing noisily. He wiped his wet lips. 'That was the only time the fire brigade came, and it had burned itself out by the time they arrived.'

'I love the pigs,' Elizabeth said to Allan at dinner. She was quite drunk now, having refilled her glass after he left her in the courtyard. She'd taken it upstairs with her, setting it on the toilet while she gave Anna her bath.

Tonight they were sitting inside, in the long white room attached to the back of the house. The French windows were open; the mauve air, smelling slightly of the pine trees planted behind the pond, drifted around them.

'Have some ham,' he said, nodding at the plate in front of her. 'Fresh from the farm.'

'No, thanks.'

'She doesn't eat it,' said Ross, and Elizabeth braced herself. They had not spoken since their scene by the pond.

'They eat everything up here,' said Allan. 'They have a pig slaughtering day and they eat the snouts. Toast them over the fire on a stick.'

'Might as well eat the snout if you're going to eat the rest of the pig,' said Elizabeth. She pulled her chair closer to the table, so that it squawked on the tiles.

Allan was not listening. 'It's a horrible business,' he said. 'They scream like anything, although Loli says the fear helps the blood pump out properly. For the blood sausage.'

'They must put up quite a fight,' said Ross, taking a gulp of wine.

'Oh, they do,' said Allan. 'They weigh more than twenty stone. It takes about six men to get one onto the killing table.'

'At least it's done here,' said Elizabeth. 'At least the pigs aren't carted halfway across the country in a truck first.'

'That's true,' said Allan reasonably. He refilled Ross's glass. 'Then when its throat's slit an old lady from the village catches the blood in a bucket. That's something to see. And she has to keep stirring the blood with her arm to stop it congealing. Like a horror movie.'

Across the table Loli sat, still silent. When Elizabeth looked at her she turned her face away.

Allan wanted to take Ross and Elizabeth touring; he wanted to drive around with them and show off the surrounding countryside. 'We could go into town,' he said, 'or down to Seville. Let's go to the corrida. There'll be one on this weekend.'

'Elizabeth's not really into bullfights,' Ross said, glancing at her.

'Why not?' said Allan, turning to her. 'You'll eat the snout.'

'I'd eat the snout if I was eating the rest of the pig,' said Elizabeth. 'But I'm not coming to a bullfight.'

'How about if I pay?' said Allan.

'It's not about *money* –' Elizabeth began, but Ross interrupted her, saying, 'Actually, I think it would be good –' and Allan caught at the end of his sentence, saying, 'It would. We'll go as a family. I'd like to treat you.'

'Ross –' said Elizabeth, but he gave her such a look that she sank back into her chair. Even drunk, she could see that he was pushing it because he was angry with her. She knew he did not really care whether she came to the bullfight. She tried to catch Ross's eye again but he kept his face resolutely turned away.

'People make too much of a fuss about it,' said Allan, wincing slightly as he adjusted himself on his hard chair. 'It's just a bull. It doesn't care.'

'That's what I think,' said Ross. 'What's the difference? Abattoir, bullring. It'll die anyway.'

'Allan is not well enough to go to the bullfight,' said Loli suddenly. They all looked at her. 'He can't sit in the sun for so long.'

'Don't be stupid,' said Allan. 'I can sit in the shade.'

'You're too sick,' said Loli. She laid her fork and knife decisively across her plate.

'Maybe she's right, Dad,' said Ross. 'Maybe it's too much.'

'I'm *fine*.'

No-one said anything for a moment, and then Loli stood up. She gestured for Ross to hand her his plate, then took Elizabeth's and Allan's. When she had gone out Allan said, 'We'll see one in Seville. Not tomorrow – I've got to see the doctor. Saturday.'

'But I don't want to,' said Elizabeth.

'They're not scared of death, here,' said Allan. 'It's a part of everything. You embrace it.'

'Really?' said Elizabeth.

'It's quite an experience,' said Allan. He nodded at Ross. 'We won't see a local one. The matadors aren't so good. It can take a long time and get a bit –' he paused, 'messy.'

Elizabeth stood up suddenly, so that her knee hit the table and made the glasses ring. 'Sorry,' she said. 'I'm not feeling very well. I think I need to go to bed.'

When Ross came to bed Anna was asleep in her cot and Elizabeth was sitting up with the lamp on, staring out at the black windows and the reflection of her face. She was still drunk, but the time spent alone in bed had made her shoulders and jaw rigid with rage. She said nothing, watching Ross take his clothes off and dump his boots on the floor.

He got into the bed beside her, making it sag so that she had to sit up straighter. He settled himself and turned his back on her. 'Don't stay up too long,' he said. 'I'm buggered.'

Elizabeth did not answer.

A minute passed, and Ross, with his back still to her, said, 'Are you going to switch the light off?'

'Fuck you,' said Elizabeth.

Ross turned over and sat up in one movement. 'Why?' he said.

'I hate you,' said Elizabeth, trying to keep the shake out of her voice. She could feel the blood in her wrists and throat. 'And I'm not coming to a fucking bull-fight, you *arsehole*.'

'Keep your voice down,' he said. They could hear Allan and Loli in their bedroom, not talking, but moving around, switching the lights off, pulling the curtains. Ross snatched the sheet up as it began to slide off the bed, glaring at her. 'You can drop your principles for once, and come.'

'I'm not coming,' said Elizabeth.

'You are bloody coming. Have some fucking manners. He's dying.'

'I don't care,' said Elizabeth.

'You are such a bitch,' said Ross, and Elizabeth found herself making a fist and swinging at him, so quickly that he could not stop her. She hit him on the shoulder, jarring her arm right down to her elbow, and then tried to hit him in the face, but by now he had hold of her hands and was forcing them back, his eyes on fire with anger. 'Don't you fucking dare,' he hissed.

'Leave me alone! Let go!' Elizabeth was frantic, gasping for breath, a shriek in her ears as she struggled and kicked out at him, dragging the sheet off them both. But he was too strong for her, and was on top of her in a second, sitting on her flailing legs and still holding her wrists in his bruising hands.

'Stop it!' he said.

She tried to shove him off, panic thrashing through her body. She struggled and twisted until her skin burned against his. His elbows thumped into her breasts as she arched and kicked and tried to wriggle out from under him, but he was too heavy and too strong and the panic and rage began to feel utterly beyond her control. She was opening her mouth to scream at him, to scream *Get the fuck off me*, when Ross shook her wrists again and leaned his face down to hers, just as Richard had done, to say, 'Stop it! You'll wake Anna!'

And instantly she gave up, her body going slack.

He waited a second, to see if she was going to fight again, then let go of her wrists and climbed off her. Elizabeth turned over straight away, face down, clutching the pillow and trying to hide from Ross. She could feel the hot skin on her arms where Ross had held her, and the pain in her knuckles from hitting him. Suddenly she was crying very hard, her cheek against the stiff cotton. She pulled her legs up under her, kept her face turned away, and cried and cried.

Then Ross put his hand on her back. It was not a hard hand. It was gentle, the fingers warm and heavy on her shivering, burning skin.

'Hey,' he said.

She could not speak or stop herself crying.

'Hey,' he said again, but still she didn't answer.

Ross stroked her back. He had not touched her like this for weeks. 'Come on,' he said, 'turn over so I can talk to you.'

His voice was soft. She lifted her face, peered up at him, sniffing and choking.

'Come on,' he said again. 'Turn over.'

She did so, scrambling into a sitting position, holding the pillow over the front of her body and looking at him through the hard rain of tears.

'Don't hit me,' said Ross. 'Okay? Just don't hit me.'

Elizabeth stared at him, wiping her eyes and gasping.

'It's not fair,' he said. 'You know I can't hit you back.'

'Why not?' Her breath was still making her chest heave.

'Because I'm stronger. You might get hurt,' said Ross.

Elizabeth continued to stare at him, the tears gathering and falling. 'I'm not coming to the bull-fight,' she said.

'We'll talk about it in the morning,' said Ross. 'I don't think we should talk about it now.' He looked at her. 'Okay?' He began to settle himself back down into the bed, and Elizabeth hugged the pillow tighter against her chest and said, 'I was raped.'

Ross stopped, the sheet halfway up his body. 'What?'

Now Elizabeth could not have prevented the tears from streaming down her cheeks. 'Not really raped,' she sobbed. 'We just had a fight, because I wouldn't have sex. I started it. I pinched him, and he hit me.'

'Who?' Ross was white. He moved towards her but she took one hand away from the pillow and held it out, stopping him, not letting him touch her.

'It's not a big deal,' she said. She used the palm of her outstretched hand to wipe her face. 'Sorry. It's not such a big deal.'

'What do you mean, it's not a big deal?' said Ross. 'Who did it? When?'

'Years ago,' said Elizabeth, and gave another gasping sob. It felt as though all the strings and knots that had held her together were coming apart. She was falling out through her own skin. 'That guy I went out with.' She brought the pillow up to her wet face, so that she couldn't see him anymore. 'I'm sorry,' she wept into it, 'I'm really sorry.'

She felt Ross climb off the bed and come round to sit next to her. She kept her face in the pillow. She heard him say, 'Why didn't you tell me?' but she could not answer.

*

In the morning they lay in the bed, their bodies touching, listening to Anna wake up. Ross asked Elizabeth to describe again what had happened.

'I'm glad you finally told me,' he said, when she had finished. It was much easier the second time. In the morning, it did not seem so shameful.

'It's a relief,' said Elizabeth.

'Still, I don't think it's really why you don't want to have sex.'

Elizabeth stopped. 'What do you mean?'

'Don't freak out,' said Ross, nudging her with his thigh. 'I just think there's more to it.'

'A lot of women lose their libido after they have a baby,' said Elizabeth, thinking as quickly as she could.

'Of course they do. I know they do,' said Ross, but he said it gently. 'You don't have to keep making excuses.'

'I thought you wanted excuses,' said Elizabeth.

'I just want you to think about it. About how important it is to us.'

Elizabeth paused. She tried to slow down – tried to let an answer, a real answer, come to her. 'Being – close? Is that what you mean?'

'Yeah.' Ross took her hand. They both watched the ceiling; the leaves and sunlight outside had begun to weave a pattern across it. 'Telling me about – what happened – is part of being close, I think.'

They had been speaking softly, but Anna was waking, and she heard them. The rustle of sheets and the little breathy voice, and there she was, appearing at

175

the edge of her cot, beaming at them, delighted to wake again and see such beloved faces.

Ross leaned over and lifted her into the bed between them and she lay there with her hands in their hair, staring at the shifting ceiling and listening to them talk. Later on she giggled as her parents reached across her to touch each other. She turned on her side so that Ross could put an arm over her and Elizabeth.

There was no talk of the bullfight at breakfast that morning. Allan did not appear to notice Elizabeth's face, which was, she knew, swollen and pale. He was preoccupied, and pale himself, and sweating.

Loli was the last down, eating a piece of toast as she stood by the table. 'We are late,' she said to Allan. 'Your appointment is at ten.'

Allan looked up at her, and Elizabeth saw Loli's face soften. She put a hand out to him and helped him to his feet.

'We will be back for lunch,' said Loli.

Heat rises, and there was no breeze that day, so the upstairs rooms would not cool down, even with their windows flung wide. They climbed the stairs to their tiled room at siesta time, Ross in front, Anna slung over one shoulder. She grinned drunkenly at Elizabeth as she was bounced upwards. Ross's hair, grown out, curled against her cheek. Elizabeth had to hold on to the wooden railings for support, her thighs weak with tiredness, and the endless heat.

The mountains were silent: a pure, clear, green silence, except for the single voice of a sheep calling to its mates as they wended their way through the cork trees and, occasionally, a corresponding clang from the bellwether.

Ross put Anna into the cot and then lay on the bed, fishing around beside him for the Dick Francis novel he was reading. This was the sixth he had read since they'd arrived, finishing each one in a day or less. Allan had a whole shelf of them in the cabinet under the tv.

Elizabeth lay down beside him, her skin damp with sweat. Their shoulders touched, and they turned their heads to look at each other.

'You okay?' said Ross.

'Yeah,' said Elizabeth.

Ross turned back to his book, held high above his head. Elizabeth lay there, feeling the deep, liquid exhaustion that comes after a storm of tears. She shut her eyes and in an instant felt the world dropping backwards, turning over, as she was tipped, safely, into sleep.

She woke an hour later, and sat up, dizzy with sleep and heat, and slid off the bed. She needed to piss – now. Ross had put Anna between them and fallen asleep himself but Anna was awake, silently watching the whiz of the ceiling fan. Elizabeth crossed the tiles quickly, before she could make a fuss. Turning into the corridor, she ran straight into Loli.

'Oh!' She began to speak but Loli put a finger to her lips, tilting her head towards the stairway. 'He's asleep,' she hissed. She pronounced it *aslip*.

Elizabeth nodded. She followed Loli down the corridor, staring at her flowered dress and her brown legs. Loli stopped at the white door of the bathroom, turning back to Elizabeth. 'Do you want to go first?' she said.

'You go,' said Elizabeth, feeling the clutching in her bladder. She must have had three glasses of wine at lunch, and water as well.

Loli shook her head. 'I'll go downstairs.'

Elizabeth could do nothing but nod gratefully and slip past her, pulling down her underpants as she reached the toilet, just in time.

They took Anna into town. 'I don't think he is going to die, you know,' said Ross, coming up behind Elizabeth. They stood in one of the town's three churches. It was dim and cool, its altar hardly visible through the shrouding shadows. In a wooden cage to their right – protected from the people – was a statue of Jesus, his halo picked out in gold and white, his face lugubrious, his plaster tears an oily blue.

Elizabeth took Ross's hand. 'Not at all, you mean? Or not while we're here?'

'Not at all. Until he's old.'

'Shall we pray for him?' Elizabeth nodded towards the altar.

'To die or to live?' said Ross.

'Aren't you the hard man,' said Elizabeth, but Ross ignored her. They stood a while longer, enjoying the quiet, until an old woman came in to pray.

They pushed the stroller out, shielding their eyes as they bumped down the steps into the dazzling white street. Elizabeth was still weak-kneed from crying; she staggered a little as they hit the pavement.

'I'll come and light a candle if he does die,' said Ross, pulling Anna's sunshade over her.

'That should help.'

'It's too fucking hot,' said Ross. 'Let's go home and have a beer.'

When they got back there was still no-one around, although the Renault was there. They went into the kitchen to boil Anna an egg. Ross pulled the fridge open. 'There's plenty of beer here,' he said.

'Shouldn't we wait for the others?'

'Who knows where they are? They could be hours.' He took out an egg, passing it to Elizabeth, and a bottle of San Miguel.

Loli appeared in the doorway, making them both jump.

'Shit! Sorry,' said Ross. 'Is it okay if I – ?' He waggled the bottle of beer.

'Of course,' said Loli. 'Allan is sick.'

Ross had opened a drawer, searching for the bottle opener. He looked up. Elizabeth turned around from the stove.

'Worse, you mean?' said Ross.

'Yes.' Loli paused. 'I don't think he will come downstairs tonight.' She did not look tired, or sad. She wore her caramel hair scraped back from the sharp planes of her face.

'He seemed alright this morning,' said Ross. He found the bottle opener and pried open his San Miguel.

Elizabeth bent over to pick up Anna, who was tugging at her dress.

Loli put her hands on her hips and looked straight at Ross. 'He is not alright,' she said. 'His kidneys are not working. He is not eating.'

'I'll come up and see him,' said Ross, putting the bottle of beer down on the table.

'Later,' said Loli. 'He is aslip.'

Ross sat with Allan the next morning. He was not well enough to come down for breakfast, and did not want to go to the hospital. Nobody spoke about the plan to see the bullfight. Loli ate breakfast quickly, leaving Elizabeth to clear her own dishes. The morning sunlight surged into the dining room. Anna ate patiently, opening her mouth every time the spoonful of cereal was aimed at her.

After she had cleared the table and done the washing up – the first time she had been allowed to – Elizabeth put Anna in the stroller and started off down the drive, heading for Paulo's place and the pigs. Her arms and back were aching from carrying Anna everywhere. She remembered how she had looked at women with babies in their arms, how it seemed so comfortable and easy. The first time she had held Anna as a newborn, she had thought, how tiny! What a feather she is! The muscles in Elizabeth's upper arms had hardened permanently in those first few months.

She hadn't walked this way before. She passed the place where the drive forked and led back up to the road. Her sandalled feet were coated in yellow dust. She leaned over and broke a little branch off a chestnut tree and gave it, wavy with leaves, to Anna.

There was a white stone goatshed by the drive, about fifty metres from Paulo's house. As they approached, Elizabeth could hear the cries of a goat; getting closer, it was possible to tell that it was a kid. There were no windows in the goatshed. Elizabeth stopped, and looked around. The little goat sounded like it was weeping.

'Don't worry, goatie,' said Elizabeth, feeling ridiculous, and the goat lifted its voice, calling to her. Anna looked up at her mother, still clutching the chestnut branch.

'Just a goat,' said Elizabeth to her. Anna grinned.

'Come on, we'll go and see the pigs.' Elizabeth squared her shoulders, head down, and pushed the stroller on, away from the weeping goat.

Paulo and Loli were standing on the steps outside Paulo's house, talking. They turned around as they heard Elizabeth approaching. Paulo smiled.

'We came to see the pigs,' said Elizabeth, and Paulo nodded, gesturing graciously towards the wire fence.

'I heard – I heard the little goat in the goatshed.'

Paulo did not understand her, but Loli said, 'Its mother is dead.'

'Oh!' said Elizabeth. 'What happened to it?'

'A dog attacked her. We had to kill her. Her baby was bitten too.'

'Is there a vet?' said Elizabeth.

Loli translated for Paulo and he smiled. He did not look much like his sister. His hair was black and he had a wide, cheerful face where hers was bony and spare.

'I,' he said, pointing to his chest.

'Paulo will look after it,' said Loli.

Paulo nodded. Anna waved her leafy stick. They all stood there for a moment, saying nothing. Then Elizabeth said, 'Loli, can I help you with Allan? Is there something I can do? Will you let me cook – or something?'

Loli looked surprised, but she smiled – the only time Elizabeth had seen her do so. '*Gracias*,' she said. 'I will tell you when.'

It was like being blessed. Elizabeth smiled back, feeling a softening in the stiff muscles of her neck, and Anna reached out to her, rattling the leaves on her stick. Elizabeth picked her up. Loli and Paulo turned back to their conversation, and Elizabeth carried Anna over to the wire fence.

There was just one pig today, a sow, lying asleep against the fence. One side of her belly was exposed, with its row of wrinkled black nipples. They flopped. They looked as though they had been sucked a great deal.

Anna leaned forward, out of Elizabeth's arms, towards the pig. 'Careful!' said Elizabeth, as she pushed her stick against the pig's leathery side. But the pig did not wake. Her long black mouth curved slightly in sleep, as though she was smiling. You could see three of her teeth, old, worn and yellow.

That night Ross sat up late, finishing the Dick Francis book. Elizabeth had been waiting for him to come to bed, for once unable to sleep until she could drape an arm across him. She slid out from the sheet, tiptoeing across the floor, and ran softly downstairs. The tiles were still warm from the day.

Ross closed the book as she came up behind him. She laid her hands on his shoulders and bent her face down to smell his hair. He took her hand and pulled her round to sit next to him on the couch.

'What happened in the end?' said Elizabeth, nodding at the closed book.

Ross smiled. 'Every single one's exactly the same.'

Elizabeth leaned against him and closed her eyes. 'It sounds kind of restful.'

'It is. The hero's always very stoic.'

'Must be why Allan likes them so much.'

It was late morning, and for lack of any other entertainment Elizabeth had been down to see the baby goat. It lay on its side, panting, and struggled away if they came close. Its wound was open, dirty at the edges, the skin dried and curling like leather. Squatting in front of it, with Anna breathing in her ear, Elizabeth felt as though she did not care if it lived, if it died, if it lay in agony for weeks. It was just a goat, and this was a bad world to be living in. Anna was bored, scrabbling to be put down. Elizabeth stood up on aching legs and the walls of the goatshed swung around her. She waited a moment to steady herself and carried Anna outside into the screen of never-ending sunlight. The little goat bleated desperately as she walked back up the dusty drive.

Ross was coming down from Allan's room as Elizabeth walked in the door. 'Hello, sweetie!' he said, putting his hands out for Anna. She grinned and reached for him as Elizabeth handed her over.

'How's your dad?' she said.

'He's asleep,' said Ross. 'Let's go for a little walk.'

'Not far,' said Elizabeth, 'we've already been on one.'

'Just out to the pond,' said Ross.

The geese were not there, for some reason, and the cicadas were quiet. They sat down on the stone steps.

'He's really on the way out. It's happened so fast,' said Ross, settling Anna on his knees.

'Was it like this with your mum?'

'No. It took her ages.'

They tipped their heads back to watch as three swallows dashed past.

Elizabeth opened her mouth, closed it, and then decided to speak. 'Have you talked to him yet?'

'What about?'

'About all the –' Elizabeth waved her hand – 'about your past. All the stuff that happened between you.'

There was a silence. Then Ross said, 'No. I told you, I don't really want to.'

'Are you sure about that?' said Elizabeth.

Ross was not looking at her. 'Well. I know he was an arsehole. He knows he was an arsehole.'

'I think it's a good idea to talk to him about it. You can leave these things too long. I just found that out.'

'This is different.'

Elizabeth felt a surge of irritation. 'Next thing you know you'll be telling me it wasn't his fault.'

'Maybe it wasn't.'

'Maybe it was your mother's,' said Elizabeth.

'Maybe,' answered Ross.

Elizabeth snorted.

'I'm being *sarcastic*,' said Ross. He pushed the hair away from Anna's eyes, making her wriggle with annoyance.

Elizabeth crossed her arms on her knees and rested her chin on them. 'No-one deserves to be hit, you know,' she said. 'That's what you said to me.'

'I know,' said Ross, his voice thin as a wire. 'But not everyone hangs around for fifteen years letting their kid get beaten up.'

Elizabeth paused. 'I hadn't thought of that,' she said. She paused again, but could not stop herself, and said, 'So you're not going to say anything?'

'He's *dying*,' said Ross.

In a rush Elizabeth said, 'I just don't know how you two can pretend nothing ever happened. How can you even look at him? If I was you I wouldn't be able to be in the same room with him! I don't get it! Say something to him!'

'There's no point,' said Ross.

'There is a fucking point,' said Elizabeth, beginning to stand up. 'He shouldn't be allowed to get away with it. It's fucking outrageous. *I'll* say something to him.'

'Don't you dare,' said Ross, and put a hand on her arm, gripping it, pulling her back down. Anna's feet slid to the ground, and she stood against him, looking up into his face.

'I could kill him,' said Elizabeth.

Ross took his hand away. 'He'll be dead soon anyway.'

Elizabeth had no answer. There was a small moment of silence and then Ross said, 'I wonder where the geese are,' but Elizabeth kept her face bent, not looking at him.

'You're in a good mood, aren't you.' He got to his feet, hoisting Anna onto one hip.

Elizabeth remained squatting where she was, still not turning to look at Ross as he trudged back to the house, Anna in his arms. She imagined herself confronting Allan, the way she had, in the earlier years, imagined herself confronting Richard. But all she could imagine, as always, was more violence. She would swing at Allan. She would smash something over his head. Bastard. Lying there, pretending he had never done anything wrong.

*

Allan came down that night, with Loli on one side and Ross on the other, and Elizabeth hovering at the foot of the stairs. Two days had wrought a terrible change in him. His face, though still ruddy, had become sunken. He had jowls. His sparse grey hair was uncombed; it was greasy and snarled at the back. And he wore a dressing gown, hanging in folds from his suddenly wasted body.

They settled him on the couch in front of the television with a glass of wine and the remote control. Ross sat next to him, and Loli disappeared into the kitchen. Elizabeth was left standing by the couch.

After a moment she said, 'I think I'll go and help Loli.'

'Okay, babe.' Ross did not take his eyes off the enormous screen. 'We're gonna watch the soccer.'

Loli was chopping onions and garlic with a huge, wooden-handled knife. She did not hear Elizabeth come in. For a second Elizabeth stood there, one hand on the door, watching.

'Loli,' she said. Loli did not hear her over the banging of the blade on the chopping board. 'Loli!'

Loli turned around. She raised her eyebrows.

'Can I help you with something?'

Loli's hands dropped to the chopping board, the knife falling onto its flat side. She looked around the kitchen.

'What are you making?'

'Paella,' said Loli. 'Not with meat,' she said, seeing Elizabeth's expression, 'prawns.' She pointed to a newspaper bundle on the big marble-topped table. 'You can peel the prawns.'

Elizabeth sat down at the table and pulled the bundle towards her. She unwrapped it. The prawns were not cooked; their curdled insides showed through their shells. They had long, whiskery antennae.

'Leave some with the heads on,' said Loli, 'for decoration.' She bent down and opened a cupboard. 'Here is a bowl.'

The prawns were prickly. Elizabeth pinched their heads off and used her fingernail to dig out the long grey thread of intestine. Loli took a bottle of red wine from the rack above the fridge and opened it, quickly and easily, the cork barely making a noise. She poured two glasses, and pushed one towards Elizabeth, then leant against the bench, watching her.

'Here we call it *paella*,' she said, pronouncing the double l like a soft j. 'I usually put chicken in it.'

'How did you know I'd eat prawns?' said Elizabeth, using her fishy hand to pick up her glass and take a gulp of wine.

'I think you could kill a prawn,' said Loli, and she smiled.

Elizabeth was taken aback. She'd explained her diet to Allan one night, but could not remember Loli listening, or even being there. She was so quiet. They looked at each other.

'Do you have children, Loli?' said Elizabeth. The question surprised them both.

'No,' said Loli. 'We didn't want them.'

'But you have Paulo's children. Your nieces.'

Loli nodded. Elizabeth saw her eyes turn hard and she looked quickly away, shaking her hand to free it of a sticky piece of shell. 'Will you use saffron in this?' she said.

'*Sí*,' said Loli. Then she said, 'I did not want Allan to make a mistake.'

Elizabeth glanced up. 'Like he did with Ross.'

Loli nodded again, and sipped her wine. She said, 'We have been very happy.'

Elizabeth watched her hands as they separated a prawn's legs from its soft body. 'I think Ross is very angry about that,' she said.

Loli shrugged.

'He's angry with you,' said Elizabeth carefully.

'It doesn't matter,' said Loli.

'It's hard for him to understand what you are going through,' Elizabeth said, pulling the tail off, trying to speak naturally. She glanced up again. Loli's eyes were bright with tears. 'I'm sorry.'

Elizabeth bundled up the prawn shells and heads and legs in the newspaper and shoved them into the bin. She washed her hands at the sink. Loli had taken down her huge paella pan, black with use. She stood over the stove, scraping and stirring.

They were shy with each other. Loli had not cried, but brushed away her tears as she took the bowl of shelled prawns from Elizabeth. Elizabeth did not know how to apologise properly for the last two weeks, for using Loli's silence as an excuse to be silent herself. She had ignorantly – and conveniently, she had to admit to herself – assumed Loli had nothing to say, since she had said nothing.

'I'll see you at dinner,' she said to Loli, turning off the tap and drying her hands on the tea-towel. 'Thank you very much for looking after us.'

Loli turned only her head, but she smiled again, and said, '*De nada.*'

The doctor arrived in the morning, pulling up outside the house in her little white Peugeot. Elizabeth was sitting on the front step with Anna on her lap, drawing patterns in the dust with a stick. Anna leaned over to look at the drawing, head bent, mouth open. Her dribble made dark loops in the dust.

Elizabeth watched as the doctor got out of her car. She guessed they must have been about the same age. The doctor wore a pressed white shirt and a brown skirt, and sandals. She had neat black hair and carried a black bag.

'*Buenos días,*' said Elizabeth, gathering Anna and standing up.

The doctor smiled. '*Buenos días.*'

'*Lo siento,*' said Elizabeth cautiously, '*no hablo español.*'

'No problem,' said the doctor. 'I come to see Señor Davies.'

'Come in,' said Elizabeth, and stepped back so that the doctor could precede her through the red doors.

Ross and Loli, who were on either side of the bed, stood up as the doctor entered. Allan lay on his back, a single pillow flat behind his head. The sheet was crumpled around his waist.

Anna wriggled and squealed when she saw Ross, putting out her arms for him. Ross shook his head at Elizabeth.

'I'll be in our room,' whispered Elizabeth, and backed out, trying to hold a now crying Anna under one arm and close the door with the other.

Anna wanted her father; her little mouth curved down at the corners; she shook her head when Elizabeth offered her a bottle of water; she smacked Elizabeth's face when Elizabeth tried to hug her. Sometimes it is not possible to think of what to do next. Elizabeth carried Anna to the bed and lay down with her on her chest, kicking, scratching and screaming until the tantrum ran out and she lay there, limp, her hand wandering to Elizabeth's hair.

'He won't go into hospital,' whispered Ross, and kneeled down beside the bed. Anna was asleep on her mother's chest, her head forced up under Elizabeth's chin.

Elizabeth rolled to one side, letting Anna gently down onto the bed. She rolled back, facing Ross. 'Will we need to hire a nurse?'

'I don't think so,' whispered Ross. 'We just have to give him morphine and keep him comfortable. It's not going to take long.'

Elizabeth's chest and neck were trickling sweat. She brought her hand up to cup Ross's cheek. 'I'm sorry I shouted at you,' she whispered.

'It's okay,' said Ross.

'I'm angry with him,' said Elizabeth.

Ross sighed. 'It'll be over soon.'

Elizabeth kept her mouth shut.

'At least Loli will miss him,' said Ross, and let his head relax into Elizabeth's hand. 'Can I get in with you two?'

Elizabeth took her first turn in Allan's room that night. It was dark; she could just make out Ross's shape as he rose from his chair and came towards her.

'He's asleep,' he whispered, and they pushed their faces together, trying to make their lips meet in the dark. Their noses bumped. Ross's breath smelt of coffee.

'Loli'll be in at about three,' said Ross next to Elizabeth's ear.

'Should I call you if he wakes up?'

'Only if he wants you to.'

Ross left, closing the door quietly behind him, and Elizabeth felt for the chair, shuffling against it and sitting down. Behind the chair was an arched window just like the one in their bedroom. She turned her head so that she could see the moon, like a fragment of shell, and, once her eyes adjusted, the furred outline of the mountains against a midnight sky.

She turned back to Allan. His breathing was slow and heavy. It was now, even in the dark, possible to tell how much weight he had lost. The sheet was folded tight across him, making barely a hillock out of his body. He choked slightly and Elizabeth leaned towards him, her foot connecting with something which seemed to leap up and crack her across the knee.

The pain shot right down the bone, and she gasped and fell back, clutching her leg, trying not to cry out. She fumbled around to see what had hurt her, and her hand found Allan's stick. That fucking stick. Someone had folded it up and pushed it under the bed. He wouldn't need it anymore.

Elizabeth held her leg and blinked back tears. Gradually the pain began to recede and her blood to slow. Allan had not stirred. She could not hear her heart anymore. Her leg ached, but she could straighten it, and bend it again. She relaxed back into her chair, her leg out in front of her, and closed her eyes.

She fell asleep, and while asleep, dreamed a familiar dream – that Rita was back, that she had never died but had been so horribly hurt by her accident that fifteen years were needed for her to recover. In this dream Elizabeth was the only one of their friends who hadn't known that Rita was sequestered at her mother's house, recovering from her injuries. And indeed, her face looked wrong, as if the healing had not been complete – it was white and vaguely shaped, as though the features had been pushed around it.

Elizabeth woke with sore shoulders, and when she tried to move her leg, it was stiff. Allan was still asleep, unmoving. The presence of Rita was like a taste; she had as good as been there, in the room. Elizabeth did what she usually did; she shook off missing Rita, she shrugged away the sense of her. It did no good, to miss her – she had been gone so long.

They took Anna into town for a change of scene. She was so overtired that she fell asleep as soon as she was put in the stroller or the car, and woke hot and confused, wanting only to be in Elizabeth's arms. They parked the car in a cobbled sidestreet, in the shade, and sat there with the airconditioning on, waiting for her to wake.

Elizabeth twisted around to look at her. She had her bottom lip thrust way out, her head dropped sideways into the car seat. Ross turned too. 'Beautiful,' mouthed Elizabeth, and he nodded.

It was market day. People streamed across the plaza. There were rows of long tables, shaded with blue plastic. They had been to the markets before; there was little to buy that could not be bought at a discount shop in Sydney. 'What do you want to do?' said Elizabeth, once they had Anna out of the car and into her stroller.

Ross put his hands on his hips. A group of teenage girls pushed past in hotpants and singlet tops, screaming and laughing. 'Fuck knows,' he said.

It was Elizabeth's turn again. She sat looking out of Allan's window. The air was so clear and the sun so bright that the green mountains seemed to be levitating, shimmering in the air. She felt like a bowl of bright fish, as though movement and colour floated through her. She took a deep breath.

Now Allan was awake, and watching her. The doctor had made an incision in his chest and inserted a tube through it and into a vein. Through the tube they injected morphine, whenever he asked for it.

'How are you feeling?' said Elizabeth, looking around her for the syringe.

'Alright,' said Allan in his thinned voice. Some-one – Loli – had combed the hair back from his face so that it fell in curls, grey and thin, on the pillow. He was sinking, it seemed, deeper into the bed. His cheeks were pale, and tinged with blue. He smelt of medicine.

He moved his fingers on the sheet.

'This?' said Elizabeth, holding up a plastic vial of morphine.

He shook his head slightly.

'A drink?' said Elizabeth, and Allan shook his head again.

'Should I get Loli?'

'Ross,' said Allan.

'He'll be up soon,' said Elizabeth. She held her breath as she leaned closer to Allan; the smell that came from him was dark and strong.

'Now,' said Allan, gasping a little. 'Important. I need to talk to him.'

Elizabeth felt her blood stop. It had come. The moment had come. 'I'll get him,' she said. She backed towards the door. 'Wait. I'll be as quick as I can.'

She ran quietly down the tiled steps, not wanting to wake Anna from her nap. Ross was in the living room, watching cartoons on tv; he turned around as Elizabeth rushed up behind him and caught at his shoulders.

'He wants to talk to you,' she said breathlessly.

'What do you mean?' he said.

'He said he wants to talk to you. He asked for you specially.'

Ross got to his feet, staring at her. 'What does he want?'

'Something important. He *asked* for you,' said Elizabeth. 'Go up. He's waiting.'

Ross left the room quickly and she heard him going up the steps. She sat down on the couch and looked at the screen, without seeing or hearing. She could not have heard what was happening in Allan's room, but her whole body strained towards it, her heart beating hard.

A minute passed, two minutes, and then Elizabeth heard a sound above the squawking cartoon; the noise of a door being slammed, so hard that she could feel the tremor in the ceiling above her. She turned around as Ross appeared at the foot of the stairs, his face white with rage.

'Fucking *arsehole*,' snarled Ross, and Elizabeth said, 'What?' getting to her knees on the couch and holding her hands out to him, but Ross kept coming, passing her, saying, 'Fucking, *fucking* arsehole.' There was a ceramic plate on the little table next to the lounge; Ross snatched it up and hurled it onto the tiled floor so that it smashed. Then he picked the table up and threw it across the room, crashing it against a wall, one of its legs breaking. He blundered over to the bookcase and began pulling books off the shelves, flinging them behind him without looking. He swept an ashtray and a bronze statuette onto the floor; he pulled a watercolour off its hooks and smashed it over his knee, and he grabbed a teacup and turned to throw it against the wall, when Elizabeth, who had been shouting it, louder and louder, shrieked, 'ROSS!'

Ross stopped, his hand still raised, and stared at her.

'You'll wake Anna!' said Elizabeth, and Ross hurled the teacup at her as hard as he could. She ducked; it missed her and broke against the far wall.

'What happened?' said Elizabeth.

'I'm going to fucking kill him,' said Ross, 'I'm going to put a pillow over his head,' and started back towards the stairs, but Elizabeth was on her feet now, catching at his t-shirt, wrenching him to a halt. They could hear Anna crying from her bedroom; from Allan's room, no sound.

'Go on then,' said Ross, panting, 'go and get the baby.'

'Just hang on. Tell me what happened.'

Ross shook his head. 'No. You won't believe it.'

'Just tell me.'

He pushed Elizabeth back with one hand. 'He said he *forgives* me.'

Elizabeth grabbed the couch for balance, staring at him. 'For what?'

'For not trying to find him after Mum kicked him out. For not keeping in touch. For not telling him about you, or Anna.'

'You're kidding.'

'He wants to die knowing that we're friends.' Ross stepped back, his shoe crunching on a piece of china. 'Bastard. I thought he was going to *apologise*.'

Anna screamed. They could hear her banging against the sides of her cot.

'I'll get Anna. I'll come back. We'll go for a walk.'

Ross leaned on the wall and turned his shoe up to pick the piece of china off the sole. 'Look what I've done. What am I going to say to Loli?'

'I'll help you clean up. Just wait.'

When Loli came home from doing the shopping they had finished sweeping the floor and throwing away the broken china. Ross had found some glue and was kneeling over the little table, trying to fix its leg back into place. Elizabeth sat breastfeeding Anna on the couch.

'What happened?' said Loli, putting her shopping bags down. Ross and Elizabeth glanced at each other.

'I lost my temper,' said Ross. 'I'm really sorry. I broke some stuff. I'll pay for it.'

'Did you have a fight?' said Loli.

'I had an argument with Dad. Then I lost it and broke everything,' said Ross. He pressed the leg into place, holding it firm. He looked at Loli. 'It was his fault.'

Loli went upstairs to see Allan, who had been left alone since Ross had slammed his door. Elizabeth propped Anna on the couch to watch tv, and she and Ross took the shopping bags into the kitchen, where they unpacked, putting things away in the unfamiliar cupboards as best they could, speaking to each other in low voices.

'What do you think he'll say to Loli?' said Elizabeth.

'I've got no idea,' said Ross, crushing an empty plastic bag between his hands. 'And I really don't care. Maybe she'll chuck us out and we won't have to see it through.'

'I don't think she will.' Elizabeth opened the fridge to put the milk in. She stared into the yellow-lit interior and said, 'I was sure he was going to apologise.'

'Even I thought that, for a second.'

Elizabeth shut the door and turned to face him. 'I shouldn't have pushed it, I'm sorry. I couldn't stop myself.'

Ross shrugged, holding out a packet of rice. 'You had your reasons.'

'I hate him. I really hate him.'

'Where do you think this goes?' said Ross.

'Top shelf.'

Ross stood on a chair to put the rice away. 'I hate him too. But it's better. Before, I kind of felt sad for him. This feels *much better*.'

Elizabeth stepped over and hugged him round the legs. She put her cheek against his hairy knees.

Ross patted the top of her head, saying, 'I should have known he wasn't going to say sorry. Some people are just bastards, and you can't do a fucking thing about it.'

Loli came down for dinner. Elizabeth cooked, using the fish that Loli had bought from the market in town, and peas that she and Anna had picked from the garden. She fried potatoes in the virgin olive oil that sat in a huge jar by the stove.

'Australian food,' said Loli, spearing a piece of fish with her fork.

'Sort of,' said Elizabeth.

'You must have missed Spanish food when you lived in Sydney,' said Ross to Loli.

She looked at him, surprised that he had spoken to her. 'I did,' she said.

'In the seventies Mum had to buy olive oil from the chemist,' said Ross.

Loli shook her head and laughed. 'It was *terrible*,' she said.

When they'd finished dinner they took their glasses of wine out onto the terrace. The mountains made a dark line against the violet sky.

'Did Dad tell you what he said to me?' said Ross to Loli.

She turned to face him. 'No,' she said.

'I'll tell you if you want,' offered Ross. 'I feel bad about breaking all your stuff.'

'You don't have to,' said Loli. 'Allan has forgotten, I think. We can let it go.'

Elizabeth, who had been standing behind them, touched Ross on the small of his back. She could feel his muscles relaxing under her hand.

Allan had bedsores that made a map of his back. He was barely conscious now; Elizabeth and Ross rolled him to one side while Loli peeled back the dressings, exposing wet, raw, pink flesh. They sponged his face, his hands, his feet. He was hot all the time. They cracked ice with a mallet in the kitchen and fed him little chips of it from a cup. He sat up once, after it had seemed he would never move on his own again, and found his assembled stick on the floor. He poked it at the patterned carpet, feverishly, again and again.

'What are you doing, Dad?' said Ross. Elizabeth was sitting next to him, with Anna asleep on her lap.

'I'm just rearranging these colours,' he said. Then he dropped the stick and lay down again, quickly pulling the sheet over himself. That was the last time he spoke.

At night, when Loli was sitting with him, Elizabeth and Anna and Ross lay in bed together. Anna slept, with a hand in each of her parents' hair, or her index finger moving in Elizabeth's ear, or stroking Ross's cheek. They could not talk for fear of waking her; instead, they hooked their feet together, pressing for comfort.

Allan began to breathe as though he was dying. Each breath sounded like it had been dragged through gravel.

'It's called Cheyne-Stokes breathing,' said Ross, bending over the bed. 'It'll last a day or two. Then –' He looked up at Loli, who was standing in the doorway, about to go and lie down. It was four in the morning. They had left Anna in the bed on her own, chocking the bottom half of her body with pillows and strewing the floor around the bed with quilts, in case she managed to roll off.

'Shall I stay?' said Loli. At last she looked tired. She had stopped pulling her hair back from her face. In the daylight it looked as though her skin had been stripped off and refitted, inexpertly. It sagged under her eyes. Now, in the moonlight, she looked like a ghost.

'It's up to you,' said Ross, 'I don't think it'll happen right now. I'll come and get you if something changes.'

Loli disappeared from the doorway without saying another word. Ross sat down in the chair. Elizabeth sat on the window seat. Allan snored on.

Elizabeth slipped back into bed with Anna at five am, when the dawn light was stealing up over the mountains. Anna was in the same position as she had been when they left, arms upflung, mouth open, eyes sweetly closed. There will never be anything so soft, thought Elizabeth, lowering her face to kiss her.

She woke an hour later to the sound of a shout, and running in the corridor, which she had instantly matched to a dream about apples falling from a tree, thudding to the ground around her. She stood up, checking that Anna was still asleep, and stepped into the corridor to see Loli's white nightie rippling up the stairs to Allan's room. She followed, putting one hand on the banister for balance. The tiles were cool on her bare feet.

Loli and Ross were standing by the bed. Loli had Allan's hand in hers; she held it to her breast. Her nightie was hanging open. Elizabeth looked away. Allan's breathing had slowed horribly; it was night-marish, hauling itself out of his body. Loli began to cry. Ross put a hand on her shoulder. They stood there for a moment that could not be measured, and as they did, Allan's breath seemed to reach the top of a hill; it stalled; it choked; it stopped.

'*Oh*,' sobbed Loli, and clutched Allan's hand closer to her. Ross looked up and met Elizabeth's eye; she grimaced, hardly knowing what she was doing.

Loli was speaking to Allan in Spanish. They could not understand the words, but it was clear that she was saying, *Come back*. Elizabeth began to cry too. Loli kept hold of Allan's hand, but he did not move, or breathe again. She kneeled down beside the bed. She shook her head violently when Ross started to say something.

Ross glanced up at Elizabeth. 'Let's go,' he whispered.

Elizabeth wiped her eyes and nodded. She looked at Allan. His face was empty. His skin seemed faintly purple. There was nothing else to do: Ross stepped over, put an arm around her shoulders, and they left the room.

*

The house was fresh that day, full of a breeze that had sprung up from the mountain. The air was sweet with it. The sky was adrift with clouds, so thin you could see the blue through them. In the newly cool air Anna slept long past Allan's death; long enough for them to help Loli undress him, and wash him. His body felt like a heavy bag of liquid; they tipped it to one side and Loli ran the washer up and down his skin, while his arm or leg sagged off the bed. The sheet had creased his skin deeply. They left the dressings on.

When they rolled him back one eye had fallen open, and Loli thumbed down the eyelid. She wiped the hair back from his face and smoothed his bushy eyebrows. He did not look much different from the way he had a few hours ago. His chest still looked as though it climbed and dropped with breath. The escape of person that had happened seemed barely to matter. He had the same smell: sweet about the hair and face, but stronger from his groin. Chemicals, mostly; the morphine that had tainted his breath had permeated his body. The urine that had soaked his pyjama pants smelt rich and metallic.

They dressed him, with difficulty, in a clean shirt and trousers, whose folds they tucked underneath his wasted body. Some friends would want to look at him, Loli said, before the funeral. The clouds unrolled past the window like silk scarves.

As Elizabeth helped tidy the room, clearing away the discarded syringes, the cups and straws, she thought that dying might be something like being horribly drunk. Lying in bed and trying to think coherently, speaking to yourself as if you were a child. Trying to make sense, to acquit yourself properly. Trying to make it over. And eventually the head falling back, letting go.

When Anna woke, she was sunny, delighted. She ate her breakfast happily, snuffling through a piece of toast like a little pig. Her fragile mood seemed to have resolved itself. Elizabeth took her out to play by the pond and feel the breeze on their faces. As they sat there, they saw a white flutter of reflection in the water's surface. The geese were back. They skidded into the water, flapping their great wings to steady themselves. Anna sat high in her mother's lap, clapping and shouting, and the geese inclined their long necks, graceful as swans, acknowledging the applause.

Ross was sitting at the big wooden table in the kitchen, looking at the local newspaper. When they came in he pushed the paper aside and held out his arms to receive Anna.

'I rang Andy,' he said.

'What for?' said Elizabeth.

'To tell him. To tell him that Dad died.'

'Did he know him?' Elizabeth sat on the table in front of him, glancing down at the paper. A blurred black and white picture of a bullfight.

'No. I just realised, though. I have no-one to tell. You're here. Mum's dead. I could have rung Penny, I suppose.' He took one of Anna's hands and put the fingers in his mouth. She chuckled and he said to her, 'I'm going to *eat* you!' Then he said, through his mouthful, 'I just wanted to tell someone.'

Elizabeth leaned over Anna and kissed his forehead. 'What did he say?'

'Nothing much,' said Ross, taking Anna's fingers out of his mouth. 'He's got a new girlfriend.'

That night, after Loli had gone to bed, leaving Allan to lie in state for the funeral the next day, Elizabeth and Ross sat up and watched television. There seemed to be nothing to say. Their thighs were pressed together as they sat next to each other on the couch, and drank from their glasses of red wine.

Ross had the remote control, and flicked through the channels, through weather, music, wildlife and an old movie, its characters embracing awkwardly on the edge of a bed.

'I'll see if there's any sport on,' said Ross, and Elizabeth sighed. He changed the channel. There was sport; a bullfight. He held the remote up again, but Elizabeth stopped him. 'No,' she said, feeling suddenly very clear. 'Leave it on.'

'You sure?' said Ross.

'I want to see what it's like.'

The fight was just beginning – a bull, looking young and filled with energy, charged out of the dark interruption of the gateway into the yellow dust of the ring. There was a rumble from the crowd. The bull swerved as it saw the matador, who stood still, watching, the light dancing over his sparkling suit. He began to move his cape, to shift it slightly, catching the bull's eye. He seemed to be using it to call the bull, tempting it, inviting it towards him. Alert, careful, it approached him. The matador turned, twisted; the bull wheeled and wheeled around him. The matador was quick and graceful; he thrust his hips forward as the bull appeared to pass underneath him; he leapt to one side when it seemed certain he would be caught on those glinting horns.

The matador stepped back and three riders entered the ring, their gold braided jackets shining dully in the sunlight, their horses stepping high, nervous. Each rider had a spear, decked with coloured ribbons, which he held upright beside him. The bull charged, crashing into one horse and nearly unseating its rider, but he held on, and the horse struggled away unhurt, protected by the thick padding on its belly and flanks. The riders moved in closer and closer; when they were close enough each, with a quick thrust, fixed his spear into the deep, hard muscle of the bull's neck.

Elizabeth shifted in her seat, put her glass of wine on the floor by her feet.

The bull, exhausted by its charge, stood staring, its sides heaving, as the riders galloped out of the ring, to be replaced by two men who scuttled out of the gateway like rats. They had their own weapons, smaller than the riders', like sticks, with ribbons like those that had streamed from the bull as it surged back and forth in the dust. There was a close-up of one man as he held his two sticks up like fangs. The camera moved in on the sticks – their tips were of silver metal, and hooked. The bull suddenly gathered itself and raced towards him and the man sprang into the air and brought the sticks down, savagely down, into its neck.

Elizabeth noticed that she was crying, the tears cool on her cheeks.

With every attack the bull had become weaker. It was as though colour was leaking from the healthy, glowing animal; its black gloss was dulling as its movement became slower, more deliberate. It swung its horns from side to side, but it was clearly confused, as though it could not believe what was happening. Who had planned this? It could not escape; it could not even look for escape, needing all its energy and attention for the scampering, scrambling men.

It was not taking long; this fight was near its end. The camera moved in on the bull, now standing unsteadily in a corner of the ring. First its face – a cow's face, with large mild eyes. Its head was shaggy with black hair. Its back was greasy with blood, and blood and foam dripped from its mouth. The matador re-entered the ring. He stopped, and struck a pose, staring at the bull, his red cape held in a fan behind his back.

Elizabeth waited breathlessly for the bull to plunge at the matador, but it did not. There was a long moment and then, almost reluctantly, it staggered forward a few steps, past the matador, pushing the cape aside with its nose. The matador had not needed to move. Then the bull shuffled around to face him again, the spears in its neck bouncing sluggishly.

'Are you sure you want to watch this?' said Ross. Elizabeth put a hand on his arm. 'Wait,' she said.

The bull headed stupidly for the cape once more, stumbling, brushing past the matador, who was on his knees now, waving the cape, trying to tempt or taunt the animal into fiercer action. It was a miserable dance; the bull turned, and turned again, but could not run and could not think to attack the matador rather than his cape. There was still power in those horns, but the bull had forgotten it.

Suddenly – so suddenly that Elizabeth gasped – the bull fell to its knees, its head down. The camera drew in closer; they could see that it was pissing itself, the dust underneath it becoming a puddle. The shot widened as the two men came forward and, with great effort, heaved the bull back onto its feet, where it stood, swaying, its head lowered and swinging from side to side. Blood was pouring from its wide black nostrils, mingling with the urine in the dust.

'Jesus,' said Ross.

Elizabeth forced herself to watch, crossing her arms over her breasts as the two men waved their small capes in the bull's face, trying to rouse it to some kind of action. It stared at them. It did not move. Then the matador drew his sword and the bull simply walked into it, the matador pushing the blade down between its shoulders, into its chest. It tried to lift its head, but couldn't. It swayed once more and fell, slowly, hitting the ground with a noiseless crash that sent blood and dust spraying over the matador.

The fight was over, and the network switched to another venue, and another fight, but Ross pointed the remote at the television again, turning it off. He groped beside him for his glass. Elizabeth used the back of her hand to wipe the tears off her cheeks.

'It's not *fair*,' said Ross. His voice was thin, strangled.

There was a pause. Elizabeth reached down to pick up her glass and swallowed some wine. Then she said, 'Why did you think it was going to be fair?'

They sat there in the dark, staring at their white faces in the blank screen.

On the last morning, Elizabeth stood on the stone terrace at the back of the house with Anna in her arms. Ross was in the far room at the top, sleeping in. She could hear Loli doing the washing, singing to herself in the cool, dark laundry. The cicadas had begun their scorching cries in the chestnut trees; heat seemed to rise from the ground, drying the dew in a humid, magical second.

The geese hovered in the pond, watching her, beaks nodding gently in her direction. They shifted as Anna suddenly struggled in Elizabeth's arms – a few backed away in a slight, silent flurry of water. None took their eyes off Elizabeth as she carried Anna towards them, crossing the terrace. As she came down the stone steps they began to move: soon all of them were in the middle of the pond, floating, paddling, watching.

The mud was cool on her bare feet. Anna was quiet, but Elizabeth's hip was growing sore. She bumped Anna onto the other hip and the geese broke ranks, fighting for the opposite shore, honking and quacking and shoving each other aside.

Elizabeth stood there for a long time, until her other hip was sore and her arms were aching from Anna's weight. The geese had returned to the pond from the safety of land and came to float in the water, as near to her as they dared. Anna was mesmerised, turning her head to watch them. She reached out to them, murmuring so quietly that they were not disturbed. And quite suddenly Elizabeth realised that if her arms ached, she could put Anna down.

She squatted, and lowered Anna onto the mud, which surged around her little toes. Anna smiled at the feel of it and leaned, lightly, on her mother's leg. The geese did not mind. There was a bubbly rush as one dipped its beak under for an insect. Their pale blue eyes reflected the sky.

Loli's singing stopped as she disappeared into the house; the cicadas seemed to relax and slow; a sheep's bell could be heard in the distance. Elizabeth, sick of squatting, let herself sit down in the mud. It seeped coldly into her underpants and around her thighs. It felt lovely. She relaxed. Anna stayed standing, one hand still resting on her mother, her eyes full of thought.

They left the car at the rental place in Seville, parking it in a row of others gleaming pitilessly in the midday sunlight, and flew on a local airline to Madrid. A man sat in front of them – he got on last, smiling at the air hostesses as he came down the aisle and slid into his seat. He had an elaborately curled moustache – a mustachio, thought Elizabeth – waxed into little ram's horns with pointy ends. He carried a small fluffy dog in a cage, which he stowed under his seat, forcing Elizabeth's feet back. Once they took off, he called for a cognac and lit a cigar.

Elizabeth swallowed against the roar of the plane, settled Anna on her lap with her bottle of water and took Ross's hand. He was looking out of the window.

'Hey,' she said, tugging gently at his hand.

He turned around. His face was wet with tears.

'Oh, sweetie,' she said, and felt tears starting in her own eyes.

He blinked and gulped. 'Sorry.'

'Don't be *sorry*.'

Ross had been quiet but dry-eyed over the past few days, helping Loli to tidy the house, calmly listening to the few expat Englishmen who had been Allan's friends. None of them had visited him while he was sick. They'd hung about afterwards though, drinking the rest of Allan's beer. They did not speak to Loli. Their Spanish seemed to be as sketchy as Elizabeth's and Ross's, and when she spoke to them in English they had trouble understanding her.

Loli cried when Elizabeth and Ross left. She stood on the stone steps at the front of the house as they drove away. She used one hand to prop herself against

the red doorframe. She seemed distracted – her eyes
kept wandering to the ground or to her skirt – she
smoothed it as they forced the last suitcase into the car
and strapped Anna in. When Ross started the car, she
waved. Then Elizabeth, turning round in her seat to
wave, saw her bend double to gather up the flowery
folds of her skirt and bring it to her face in a burst of
weeping.

And now Ross cried, knuckling his eyes the way
Anna did when she was tired.

'I hate this,' he said. 'He was such a bastard. He
doesn't deserve it.'

He held his arms out for Anna. Elizabeth passed
her across and he put his face into her neck. All this
time, watching Allan die, Elizabeth had been unable
to feel pity, but now it overwhelmed her. All the years
when Ross should have been free of baser knowledge,
free of worry, when he should have been a boy, swallowed up by Allan's selfishness. Blindly, Elizabeth
stroked the back of his head. She could feel the little
dog shuffling about in its cage at her feet. 'It has been
hard for you,' she said with difficulty.

'It has,' wept Ross, 'it really has.' Anna squirmed at
the feel of his warm tears on her shoulders. Cigar
smoke drifted over their heads, rich and acrid.

Ross freed one hand and tried to wipe his face. 'Am
I like him?' he said, sniffing.

Elizabeth stopped, her hand still on his curly hair.
Her heart thumped. 'Like him?' She used her hand to
turn his face so that she could see it. His wet eyes,

dark-shadowed. The stubble on his cheeks. She leaned towards him and could smell him through the cigar smoke, warm, like bread. She thought about how much she hated him when he was righteous and angry, and how good he was to Anna, and how much she loved him. How deeply generous he was with his body and his heart.

'You're not like him,' she said. 'You're lovely.'

He groped for her hand. Anna watched them, her face still and unsurprised.

Their flight home was in the evening again. It was twilight as they passed through; night by the time they had Anna settled to sleep in the plane. Ross and Elizabeth sat side by side, not bothering to talk over the plane's ceaseless roar. Ross put an arm around Elizabeth's shoulder. Elizabeth, next to the window, reached over and slid up the little plastic shutter, wondering if she would be able to see any stars. She could not. She gazed out past the reflection of her face into the formless dark.

She remembered being thirteen, staying the night at Rita's stepfather's and swimming with her in his indoor pool, which was encased in glass in his enormous concrete house. The night, like this one, had been deep outside.

They had been underwater, trying to swim two full lengths of the pool without coming up for a breath. Now they trod water, facing each other, panting. In a voice that sounded louder in the glass room, Rita said, 'I saw Neil kissing my mum. They had their mouths open.'

Elizabeth made a face.

'I'll show you,' said Rita. She ducked under again and, always obedient, Elizabeth followed her. Rita, kicking to keep herself submerged, put her two hands on Elizabeth's shoulders. It was blue and blurry under the water. The girls struggled together and kissed, with mouths open and full of water, their lips slippery and warm. Then they burst to the surface, gasping for air, smiling, blushing, and reaching for the safe sides of the pool.

Elizabeth blinked and brought her face away from the cold window so that she could look into her own reflected eyes again. It was not possible to have such safety anymore, or for a kiss to be so simple, or so sweet. It was not possible to be protected. Rita was gone, and Richard had been cruel, and stupid. Allan was dead without saying sorry. The bullfight was not a beautiful, meaningful dance, but an enactment of savagery and stupidity, like life itself. People and animals lived in fear and died in pain. And there was nothing holding the plane up but luck, and the plane itself.

Acknowledgments

Most heartfelt thanks and love to Peter Bishop, Russell Daylight and Charlotte Wood for their skill and generosity as readers.

For reading, editing and helpful conversation, thanks also to Debra Adelaide, Gavin Angus-Leppan, Joss Bennett, Anthony Blair, Sam Chesterton of Finca Buenvino, Anna Funder, Ali Higson, Jo Jarrah, Mireille Juchau, Steven Kelleher, Georgia Macbeth, Patrick McIntyre, Beth Norling, Jane Palfreyman, Cathy Sherry and Anthony Skuse.

Thanks to Mum and Dad for continuing interest and support, and love to Alice and Paddy, who made room for me to write this book.